The H

Aliyah A. Symonette

Edited by Jade Weiss

Cover Design by Tylen Perpall

www.Pinkletters.net

Also by Aliyah A. Symonette

Norfolk Street

"Those we love never truly leave us. There are things that death cannot touch."

— *Jack Thorne*

For my nephew, Isaac

Table of Contents

Part 1

Chapter 1 - Key West

"Key West. I have a new case for you!" Sergeant Knowles calls out to us.

The nickname has been around since we became partners 4 years ago and it's been a thorn in our sides ever since. I sigh at our pet name as we shuffle into the Sergeant's office.

After the briefing on the new case, Key and I head over to the morgue. We learnt the body was rushed over because of the couple's social status. The department wanted to keep the news under wraps for as long as possible.

The car ride over is short but crammed with anticipation. Even though other officers and detectives had already been to the scene, the Sergeant wanted us on the case. This could be a high-profile case; the biggest either of us has ever been assigned. The gravity of what this could mean, personally and professionally, is not lost on us. The stakes are high, but so is the reward.

Detective Key gets out of the car first, shuts the door and pulls out a cigarette. She places the cigarette between her lips and leans on the car as she fishes for the lighter in her pocket. It takes me a second to respond because Key rarely smokes. She's admitted to me in the past, on one of our long stakeouts, she only smokes to calm her nerves.

It must be the case, or could it be…

Before she can light the cigarette, I walk over and pluck it from her lips. The scent is awful and it's a bad habit she should give up.

"Are you worried about seeing her? It's been ages." I laugh as I crush the cigarette in my palm and place it into my pocket.

"I'm not worried!" Key pushes off the car and heads into the morgue. "I just needed a cigarette," she mumbles.

"It'll be okay. Let's just focus on the case." I smile knowingly as I follow her in.

"Detective West, it's good to see you." The Medical Examiner addresses me politely. She turns to Key and acknowledges her flatly, "Gray."

I cough to hide my laugh. Maybe I *should've* let Key have the cigarette.

From my understanding, the examiner and Key went on a few dates a while back, but nothing serious came out of it. Key told me it 'fizzled out' because they were both too busy to see each other. She said it ended amicably, but standing here now it doesn't feel that way. I'm putting my money on the real story being Key ghosting her. She's done it many times in the past. Unfortunately for her, this time she must work with the woman.

"It's good to see you too, Doc." I smile at the examiner and Key sheepishly nods in greeting. "What do you have for us today?"

She leads us into a cold space where our victim lay waiting in the middle of the room on a metal table. There's a large freezer, big enough to hold multiple bodies in it, and two sinks on the opposite side of the room. I notice the scale hanging above the body and a red garbage bin close by the table. A shiver runs down my spine as I observe the instruments next to the body. Coming to the morgue is one of my least favorite parts of the job.

It's lifeless. A person has been turned into a science project to be pricked and prodded at. The tag on your toe is all that's left to identify you. A dark cloud always hovers over me whenever I leave this place.

"Well let's start with the basics: The victim has been identified as Cypress Fellow. Male. Age 40. Black. 6'1 ft. 184 lbs…" She gives us more details about our victim and then, finally, gets to the climax. "Initially, I was going to classify this as an accident because of the fall." Her eyes lock on the victim as if she can see right through him. "But, after further observation, I determined the fall was postmortem. Mr. Fellow was already dead when he fell from the roof. I haven't had much time with this one, but we can classify this case as a Homicide. The COD looks to be suffocation. Mr. Fellow has bloodshot eyes, and

I found a couple of fibers on his face. I'll be sending off blood samples to be tested for his CO_2 levels. Once it's back I'll know for sure. I'd say the time of death was between 6 AM to 9 AM this morning. I'll have a full report to you in a couple of weeks."

"Thanks, Veronica. Any chance you could get it to us sooner?" Key asks. "This is an important case."

"They're all important," she answers curtly. "I'm busy right now, but I'll try my best to get it to you as soon as possible."

"Thanks, Doc. We appreciate the help; we'll get out of your way now." I step in to prevent Key from embarrassing herself further.

———————

Detective Key and I drive to the crime scene about 30 minutes away. The victim was a groundskeeper for an affluent couple living in a luxurious gated community in Brentwood, California. His body was found in their backyard.

"Wow, this is the closest I've ever been to a celebrity!" Gray pulls out a protein bar from the glove compartment box.

"They're not celebrities." I roll my eyes.

"Yes, but they work with them. The wife's a well-known psychiatrist with celebrities coming in and out her door. She's hosted more than one TED talk and has a large following on social media. The husband's a private pilot for a few famous rappers and actors. They're basically celebrities."

"Oh, whatever. Just focus on the case. The wife and husband should still be at the house when we get there. It's critical we get the most out of this initial meeting. I don't want to miss a thing. The examiner's exam isn't completed yet, so we won't be volunteering it's going to be classified as a homicide."

"Okay, okay." Key agrees as she balls the wrapper and puts it back into the glove compartment box.

I quickly give her a stern side eye before returning my focus on driving. "Let's go over the facts, shall we?"

Chapter 2 - Dead Groundskeeper

Driving up to the security gate, we show our badges to the guard and inform him which house we're going to. The guard lets us in quickly; officers and CSI have already been at the crime scene. He knows why we're here. In a community such as this one, I'm sure news of Mr. Fellow's death has already spread like wildfire.

A high-pitched whistle escapes my lips as we pass the gates of the most luxurious homes I've ever seen. These houses are owned by people who have yachts, planes, and multiple homes—things I could never afford.

"I know right? These houses are amazing." I think I see a bit of drool coming out of her mouth as Key looks out of the window in admiration.

"They're nice but I don't think I could ever live here," I confess.

My foot eases off the gas pedal so we can gawk a little longer. A small indulgence is allowed before we get to the crime scene and have to get serious.

"Why not?" Key asks. "I could see myself in one of these homes. A wife, a few kids... even a dog. That'd be the life."

"The people living in these places aren't happy. And what would I even do in a house with over five bedrooms and walk-in closets the size of a living room? It's unnecessary and obnoxious."

Key doesn't get a chance to respond as we turn onto Sakura Lane and approach the house. The first floor is mostly hidden by high cream walls which match the exterior of the house. We pass the front gate. It's crowded with reporters, neighbors, and paparazzi who managed to bribe their way in here. I stop the car at a smaller side gate. Crime scene officials flow in and out of this gate.

There's nowhere to park directly on the property. The manicured lawn is tarnished by the tire tracks of news reporters, police officers, and forensic units.

With not even enough room to make a three-point turn, I shift the car into reverse and resign to park outside the side gate. It takes an extra two minutes to make our way to the house from the street, but our demeanor remains focused. Key and I don't speak a word during the short trek. When we finally come into full view of the jaw-dropping house behind the walls Key mutters under her breath, "Damn."

Looking at the other homes on the way here was astonishing but seeing one of them up close is breathtaking. This modern, square palace has floor-to-ceiling windows on the first floor, giving a stellar view into this beautiful home. I glimpse a seating area and a floating staircase. The tall palm trees outside offer little privacy. I've never seen anything like it. This place must cost a fortune.

After we pick our jaws up off the floor, we step over the threshold of the front door, which remains propped open by a small wooden wedge. I spot the yellow tape at the back of the house through the sliding glass doors. The forensic team is still here gathering evidence. I nudge Key to head to the backyard, but we are halted by an authoritative voice.

"Hello? I haven't seen you two before. Who might you be?"

Following the voice I notice a striking woman heading towards us with an eyebrow raised in question. Her heels slap the floor as she closes the distance between us. Unable to look away, I study her.

Straight black hair is pulled into a tight ponytail hanging low at her neck and cascading down her back. A white silk button-down shirt and brown slacks hug her slim frame; she looks ready for work or a casual outing. Her dangling earrings and many bracelets complete the look. Hips sway as she steps powerfully in our direction. Her brown complexion glistens in the sun and her skin looks smooth to the touch. As she takes her last steps, I notice the exasperated expression on her face and her full lips—

I clear my throat and extend my hand in greeting, "Hello, I'm Detective West and this is my partner Detective Key. We're the lead detectives on this case and will be taking over the investigation from here."

She returns the gesture. I was right, as smooth as silk. "I'm Saloni Barlowe. My husband and I already spoke to a police officer. Is there something else you need from us?" She crosses her arms over her chest.

Key and I show our badges. "Yes, thank you for your cooperation, but we would like to ask some follow-up questions. Is your husband here?" Key extends her hand to Mrs. Barlowe, but she doesn't shake her hand. Mrs. Barlowe stands in silence for a few beats. Annoyance radiates off her in waves. Then she suddenly turns around and walks away, leaving us to follow.

"I guess these people *are* unhappy." Key whispers to me as we follow Mrs. Barlowe into the kitchen.

———————

Key and I introduce ourselves to Yael Barlowe. He's a black man of intimidating size. I would say he's about 6'4" which would make him around 3" taller than me. It's obvious he doesn't dim down his big presence and is used to doing all the talking. Mrs. Barlowe fiddles around the kitchen, avoiding conversation and eye contact with us. Dishes clank as she shuffles glassware into cabinets then moves to brew a pot of coffee.

I ask Mr. Barlowe about their relationship with the victim, Mr. Fellow.

"He was our groundskeeper and handyman for smaller fixes around the place," he tells us. "We didn't know him on a personal level, but we hired him about 5 years ago and he's always been nice enough," he pauses. "This is so sad."

Key and I exchange looks. Mrs. Barlowe swivels around—catching our silent conversation—with a cup of coffee for her husband.

"Oh, I'm sorry. I only made enough coffee for two. Do you want water?" She offers us a tight smile.

"Yes please, we'd appreciate it," I respond. "Did you spend any amount of time with him, Mrs. Barlowe?"

She grabs two water bottles from the cabinet and hands it to us.

"No, it's as my husband said, we didn't know him well."

"Okay, well can you tell us what happened this morning and what led to your phone call?" Key asks.

"We already told the other cops about this," she sighs deeply.

"It's okay honey. They're just doing their job." Mr. Barlowe places a hand on his wife's shoulder. She flinches but quickly recovers and makes herself busy in the kitchen again.

"My wife called. We had a normal evening in last night. This morning she came downstairs first and found Cypress on the ground. He'd fallen from the roof and hit his head, I guess. I came down shortly after and heard her screaming. She quickly called 911 because we didn't know how long he'd been out there. And now we're here."

"What time did you get up?" Key questions.

Despite wanting to stay engaged in the conversation, Mrs. Barlowe diverts my attention. Her fingers drum over the countertops as she absentmindedly fiddles around the kitchen and hums a song softly to herself. She hasn't spoken much since we got here but she often glances in my direction. Her husband is more willing to speak. We'll need to conduct their interviews separately if we want to get any real information from these two.

"About 9 a.m. Cypress usually starts his day at 8 a.m. I had asked Cypress to check out the roof for leaks, but I had no idea this would happen…" Mr. Barlowe takes a minute to clear his throat and compose himself. It sparks my interest when Mrs. Barlowe doesn't go to comfort her husband. She watches us intently as she leans against the counter and sips her coffee.

"Mrs. Barlowe," I address her as we hold each other's gaze. "Did you wake up at the same time as your husband?"

"Yes."

"Did either of you hear any noises this morning before you got up?"

"No, like I said, we already told the other officers everything we know," she retorts.

Mrs. Barlowe starts busying herself around the kitchen again as Key and I take turns asking questions. My eyes lock with Mrs. Barlowes a few times. There's a bit of an electric charge and I find it very hard to keep my focus in these moments. I wonder if she's feeling what I'm feeling.

She answered any question we sent her way with one word. By the time we feel satisfied with enough information to start this case any warmth she possibly offered us in the beginning is gone.

───────────

"I'll have an officer drop you both to the station where we'll take your official statements. We'll wrap up here and meet you there in a bit. We'll need a couple of days with this scene, so it's best you pack a bag to take with you. Do you have someone you both can stay with? Or are you able to check into a hotel?"

"We'll stay at a hotel near here," Mr. Barlowe responds.

"Okay, once you decide on a hotel, please let us know where we can find you. Detective Key will accompany you upstairs to get your bags and make sure an officer takes you to the station."

"Is this necessary? Following us into our room?" Mrs. Barlowe isn't happy with this arrangement. Most people aren't when we say this but whether they know it or not they're suspects.

"Sal…" Mr. Barlowe gives his wife a warning. He nods at us. Our eyes lock again before they march out of the kitchen with Key trailing behind.

Chapter 3 - That Wife is Something Else

The sound of Mrs. Barlowe's heels slapping against the floor alerts me to their departure. I rush from the backyard to catch up to the couple. There was something I hadn't thought to ask when we spoke in the kitchen.

My voice booms across the lawn as I call out to stop them. I catch up as they're getting in the car.

"Sorry, I forgot to ask you both something. Does anyone else, besides you two, have access to your house?"

They look at me strangely. Surprisingly, Saloni is the one to respond.

"Our chef and stylist have keys to the house."

"No one else? No family members?"

"No, just those two."

"Okay, can I have their names? And can you ask them both to come down to the station please?"

Mrs. Barlowe complies, and I scribble their names on my notepad.

As my pen strokes the last letter on paper, the car door in front of me slams shut. It's clear Mrs. Barlowe is not pleased with how her day is going. Key and I watch as the car speeds down Sakura Lane, disappearing from view.

———————

"That wife is something else." Key shakes her head as we head into the house.

"Hmm… I don't know. It seems like something is going on with the husband," I reflect.

"Yeah, well it's not our job to investigate marriages. Let's go back inside," Key replies.

After we inspect the backyard and first floor we head upstairs. There are 5 bedrooms and 4 bathrooms. We decide to split up and check them all. My first impression after entering the first room: They must have the best cleaning service. There's not one piece of decor out of place. No dirt or old stains on the carpet. The house is immaculate. The white walls give the place a pristine and pure look, but the mood up here feels different. There's an ominous chill crawling in my bones. It's as if I'm back in the morgue, there's no life here.

The last room I check is the master suite. A king-size bed sits in the middle of the room with nightstands on either side and long pendant light fixtures above it. There's a door leading to the massive walk-in closet. I halt at the threshold, shocked.

How could one person own this many clothes, shoes, and handbags? Almost everything in here belongs to Mrs. Barlowe. This is the only room not organized. I can tell Mrs. Barlowe comes in here often. A few pieces of clothing litter the ground, shoes off center and two bags on the small island in the middle of the room. I approach the island, noticing the glass casing with perfumes on one side and shelving on the other. There are miscellaneous objects like a measuring tape, a speaker, an unplugged night light, candles and a few other small items, but the most intriguing is a book.

A brown leather book with off-white pages and an old textured spine. The front of the book says "NOTES". Out of curiosity, I skim the pages. There are journal entries here as far back as 2 years ago. There's no name in it but it must be Mrs. Barlowe's.

There must be something in here to help us connect with Mrs. Barlowe and get her to open up to us. It's not right but this would be for work I tell myself. It could hold a necessary clue or be a way for me to leverage something against Saloni during an investigation.

I decide to do something I've never done in my entire career. I decide I'm going to take the book with me but won't file it as evidence, at least not yet. If I find something pertaining to the case, I'll turn it in. If not, I just need to put it back before anyone notices it's gone.

As much as I hate to admit it there's also a desire deep within to read this journal. Mrs. Barlowe intrigues me, and I can't deny I want to know more about her. The electric charge I felt when I first saw her was undeniable. I couldn't concentrate on our conversation with Mr. Barlowe or keep my eyes off her.

My conscience pricks at me but my sudden desire to know more forces my feet to keep moving as I leave the closet with the book in hand.

Chapter 4 – Bring in The Chef

After searching the second floor, Key and I leave the Barlowe's mansion. As we approach the car, I let out a shaky breath and rub the back of my neck. The empty and uncomfortable feeling never left the entire time we searched the house. My stomach in knots, begins to dissolve and the goosebumps on my arms start to fade away.

I am glad to be out of the house. Relieved.

———————

When we arrive at the station Key pulls out another cigarette. This time I don't stop her; I snatch one for myself. A millisecond after my first inhale I regret it. The few times I've tried smoking I didn't enjoy it. Key takes a few more drags from her cigarette as I smash mine under my shoe before we head inside.

The Barlowes, a lawyer and two others who I assume are the stylist and chef are seated out front waiting for us. There's aggravation written all over her face. I instruct Key to take care of getting their statements while I initiate the other interviews. I check my notepad and ask Ms. Dixon, the stylist, to follow me into one of the interrogation rooms.

My first impression of Ms. Dixon is she's an open and honest person. She informs me she's been working for Mrs. Barlowe for 3 years. About a year and a half ago she was given a key because there were a few incidents when Mrs. Barlowe needed her to grab an outfit. Now, she goes by the house to plan Mrs. Barlowe's outfits for the week.

Ms. Dixon is 28 years old, only a year younger than me. Her fashion style is unique but modern. The light brown curls, with blonde highlights, on her head compliment her dark skin. She's well put together and has an air of maturity to her.

She's forthcoming and pleasant to speak to. I believe her when she says she doesn't spend much time with Mr. Barlowe and never had a real conversation with the victim. There's no reason to distrust her. She couldn't have pulled this off anyway, at least not on her own. Our interview is almost over by the time Key enters the room.

"Can you tell me where you were last night and this morning?" I inquire.

"My friend, Jakob, and I went out last night. I still have a few stories up on social media." Ms. Dixon unlocks her phone and shows me. "And this morning I slept in from a hangover. Jakob slept over as well."

"Okay, do you have a contact for Jakob? We'll need to reach out to corroborate your statement."

"Wait, why does it matter? Mrs. Barlowe told me it was an accident. Mr. Fellow fell right?" She looks back and forth between Key and me.

"This is just standard procedure. We need to cover all our bases." We still haven't told the Barlowes this case is a homicide. I slide over a piece of paper and pen. "You can write his full name and number on this."

She writes the information on the paper and slides it back over to me.

"Is there anything else you can think of or would like to tell us?" Key asks.

"No, I don't," she responds with finality.

"Well thank you for your time, Ms. Dixon. Here's my card." I slide the card across the table. "Please give us a call if anything comes up."

"Will do." Key and I shake her hand before she leaves the interrogation room.

"Since I missed the interview, what did you think of her?" Key asks me.

"Once the friend can verify her movements from last night to this morning, I think we can check her off. She seemed very open and honest. There's nothing suspicious about her, she has no motive, and an alibi."

"Woah. High praise coming from you. You're usually skeptical of others." Key raises her eyebrow.

"Because I have to be in this line of work, but I'd like to think I'm a good judge of character and Ms. Dixon is no killer," I explain.

"Well okay then. Are you ready to bring in the chef? What's his name?"

"It's Jing, Lazer Jing."

"I'll bring him in." Key leaves the room to get Mr. Jing.

Chapter 5 - A Siren

On my drive home, my eyes feel heavy. I've already lost count of the number of times I've yawned. The car volume is turned up loud to keep me awake. Once I make it home safely, I practically crawl out of my car to head inside.

I shower on autopilot. Desperate to climb into my bed and sleep, but the growling of my stomach demands otherwise. Thankfully, I have leftovers in the fridge I can heat up quickly. As I eat, I replay the events of today in my head: the morgue, the Barlowes, and the interviews at the station. We were quickly able to take Mr. Jing off our suspect list as well. He had a solid alibi and no motive.

It's been a long day.

Sergeant Knowles will make a public statement soon. In the meantime, we'll have to keep the press vultures at bay. This case will be headline news tomorrow. Once the public knows this is a homicide case, not an accident, there will be loads of pressure on Key and me to solve this. There'll be a good deal of sensationalizing by the media. I sigh into my leftovers, thinking about the cameras, interviews, and journalists already at the station and the ones sure to find us over the duration of the investigation.

We suspect the Barlowes are withholding information. Their bedroom is on the other side of the house from where Mr. Fellow was found but it's hard to believe they didn't hear anything. And if they didn't, could someone be framing them?

Mr. Fellow was suffocated and then thrown off the balcony. I assume to make it look like a fall but did an altercation take place on the balcony beforehand?

His usual schedule was to get to the Barlowes around 8 a.m. Did he die shortly after getting there or did he come in a little earlier this morning?

We still don't know the circumstances surrounding Mr. Fellow's death and until we get the examiner's report, or a confession from someone, we're not allowed to make any big moves. The sergeant has already made it clear this case is to be kept as closemouthed and low-key as possible. If we mess up the whole department will be in trouble.

After washing the dishes I head into my bedroom closet to lay out my clothes for tomorrow. I step back and look at my "walk-in closet". It's really small in comparison to the closet I stood in earlier. Her closet might be bigger than my bedroom. I'm still shocked someone could have so many things. I wonder if she's filling a void—

Wait. I forgot the journal!

With a surge of energy coursing through me I race to the car and grab the journal. I left it in the car after we got back to the station, and it slipped my mind entirely. I think a part of me wanted to forget I was capable of borrowing—stealing the book.

With the journal in my hand again I feel an unexplainable pull towards it like a siren calling to me. A pull towards Saloni. I haven't opened the book yet.

The anticipation is almost unbearable. The book feels like a live wire in my hand—thrilling but dangerous.

I can almost hear the book calling out to me... drawing me in...

> Her song travels far across the sea to where I
> stay,
> safe in the sand.
> I know what sirens do; I should be afraid.
> But as her song surrounds me, my feet slowly
> make their way towards the shore.

This is not a good idea, but I can't stop myself. A part of me feels justified. We need to know the truth behind Mr. Fellow's death and if this journal can lead me in the right direction, it'll be worth it.

I'll return it in a few days. I tell myself as I get comfortable in bed and open the journal.

Chapter 6 – July in California

The shrieking of my alarm jolts me awake. A bit disoriented, I spring up and survey my surroundings; I'm in my room. A thump follows. I look over the edge of the bed to detect the cause of the disruption and see Mrs. Barlowe's journal. I don't remember when I fell asleep. As interested as I am in discovering her secrets, I was no match for fatigue. I'm not the fastest reader but I got through a couple of journal entries. There's been no mention of Mr. Fellow yet. The journal is made up of random short paragraphs, poems, and even little doodles. Some entries are only one sentence. It's a collection of random thoughts. A bit confusing but there's still a good deal more to read. I run my hand down my face as I swing my feet out of bed.

"It's time for a shave, Izaak." I tell myself.

———————

After Mr. Fellow's next of kin were properly notified, Key and I made a list of people we need to speak to over the next few days—possibly weeks. At the top of our list is another person we learned about who has access to the Barlowes' house, Moriah Estor—Mr. Barlowe's business partner. Mrs. Barlowe called this morning to inform us the partner has a spare key to the house for emergencies but has never used it, so she forgot to mention it yesterday.

The forty-minute drive to Mrs. Estor's office passes by quickly. We go over the case and agree Key will take the lead on this interview. I'm in no position to lead the interview. My conscience is eating at me. What I did was disgraceful. The guilt is making me feel queasy. I want to bring up the journal to Key but I can't. It's not the right time and I'm ashamed of my behavior.

Besides, there's no reason to mention it unless I find information pertaining to the case, right?

The heat pierces my dark skin as we step out of the car. The July heat in California is unbearable. We quickly enter the building to avoid melting and head for suite 305.

The suite is not as big as I expected. There's a small reception area in the front and a few private offices separated by a large glass wall which makes up most of the space. The white walls remind me of the Barlowes' house. I shake off a shudder as we walk up to the receptionist's desk, show our badges, and ask for Mrs. Estor. The polite receptionist checks her screen and leads us to Mrs. Estor's office.

A tall gray door opening reveals Mrs. Estor sitting at her desk across the room. She slowly gets up as the chair creaks from the loss of weight. Immediately, my nostrils are invaded with the scent of lavender. She must have a diffuser or just put out a candle. Either way, it makes for a good greeting. Key and I shake the manicured hand extended to us.

"I figured someone would reach out but not this soon. Yael told me this morning Saloni gave my name to the police. I assume you're the two detectives looking into this tragic accident?"

"Yes, ma'am. I'm Detective Key and this is Detective West," Key introduces us. "We have a few questions and were wondering if we could have a bit of your time?"

"Of course, take a seat." She points to the two chairs on the other side of her desk. She turns to the receptionist still at the door. "Xani, make sure we're not disturbed."

"Will do, Moriah." Xani, the receptionist, closes the door behind her.

"What can I do for you?" Mrs. Estor sits back in her creaking chair.

"Can you tell us about your relationship with the Barlowes?" Key asks. We pull out our notebooks.

"Yael and I are business partners. Have been for almost 10 years now. My husband and I have been to their house a few times before for dinners. We get along well but my relationship is more with Yael. Saloni mostly stays to herself."

"You've been partners for 10 years, but it doesn't seem like you're very close with the Barlowes." My curiosity piques.

Mrs. Estor shifts in her seat and tucks her hair behind her ears. "Well, Yael is very professional. Our relationship has only ever been as business partners and acquaintances."

"What about Mrs. Barlowe?" I ask. Key side eyes me for jumping in again.

"Like I said, she keeps to herself. Although I'm not sure if by choice..."

"Why would you say not by choice?" Key's finally cuts me off and takes control of the interview.

"This stays between us, right?"

"Yes ma'am," Key responds. I nod in agreement.

"Well, I don't like to gossip... but Yael can be a bit possessive and controlling. I've overheard him say some nasty things to her over the years, but she never fights back. She just plays the part of the submissive wife."

"I thought you said you weren't close?" Key questions. I'm happy I let her take over this interview. She asks all the right questions.

"We're not but I'm very observant. Over the years you notice things like hushed conversations behind closed doors or body language at a function. I never saw them as a match for each other, but I guess they make it work. I'm sorry but what does this have to do with that poor man's death?"

"This is just standard procedure. We are interviewing others with access to the house as well. Can you tell us about your whereabouts on the morning of and the night before?"

"I was home. I had a call with Yael about work and then I went to bed."

Key looks up from writing in her notebook. "Can anyone corroborate your story?"

"Yes, my husband was home and we have cameras outside of our house."

"Okay, have you ever used your key to access the Barlowes' house?"

"No, I've never needed to use it."

"Is there anything else you can tell us about the Barlowes or Mr. Fellow?" I jump in.

"No, I've only ever seen Mr. Fellow in passing, the few times I was by the house. He seemed like a nice man. This is such a tragedy."

"Thank you for your time, Mrs. Estor. We'll be in touch if we need anything else. If you think of something, please let us know." Key hands over her card.

Mrs. Estor bumps into the table as she gets up. She shakes our hands and escorts us out of the office.

Chapter 7 - The Greater Good

The week following Mr. Fellow's death was filled with interviews. We needed to speak to as many of his family members and friends as possible. From what we've gathered, Mr. Fellow was a hardworking, honest man who made a positive impact on many people in his lifetime. He had no enemies or vices. The Barlowes paid him well and he had no previous record. He left behind a wife of 30+ years and 3 kids who love him dearly. There was nothing to suggest this was a crime of passion by someone who hated him.

Although, this was no accident either. Someone suffocated Mr. Fellow and intended to kill but who would have a motive? All roads kept leading back to the same place.

The day after speaking with Mrs. Estor, the sergeant released a statement to the public announcing this case was being considered a homicide. He also introduced Key and me as the lead detectives. The media viciously began their attack. It was a hassle to leave the station and evade the crowd outside. In those first few days after the homicide announcement, we were bombarded by cameras and other media personnel trying to get a comment from us about the case.

"Do you have any suspects?"

"Are the Barlowes involved in this?"

"Who pushed him?"

"Was Mrs. Barlowe having an affair with Mr. Fellow?"

The theory the media had run with: Mrs. Barlowe was having an affair with Mr. Fellow which led to Mr. Barlowe killing him.

We aren't ruling anything out but personally, I don't believe it. Mrs. Barlowe is not that kind of person. In the past week I've been able to read the journal two more times. I'm starting to understand a little bit of who Saloni Barlowe is. She's not a cheater. When I have free time, I pick up the journal, but I need to read faster. I need to return it as soon as possible.

Fortunately, no one's noticed it's gone yet, including Mrs. Barlowe.

With the pressure on to finish, I've put the journal in my car so I can read whenever Key isn't around. I still haven't told her I took the journal. I'm not sure what her response would be, and I don't want to feel even worse than I already do.

———————

I arrive home at 7 p.m., earlier than usual. Usually, I would take advantage of this rare opportunity to get extra sleep, but the journal has been on my mind all day. It's been about 3 days since the last entry I read. At this point, I swear I can hear Saloni's voice floating around in my head. The pull leaves a heavy weight on my chest...

A dark night blankets the sky as cold sand tickles my toes.

It's impossible to see her in the distance, but her
sweet melody propels me forward.
When my feet meet the shore, I barely feel the
bite of the freezing water.
The bobbing boat in the shallow is my ticket to
her.

I forgo my routine of showering and eating when I get home. Instead, I remove my gun and plop onto the couch with the journal, picking up where I left off.

My grumbling belly pauses my reading. Peeping through my curtains I notice the sun has gone down. I check my watch; it's been two hours. Releasing a sigh I drag myself off the couch and head into the kitchen to turn on the oven. The frozen lasagna bakes while I shower and wash my hair.

The temptation to pick it back up while I eat dinner is strong. I'm halfway through the journal and I'm desperate to finish. My conscience nags me less and less each time I read. Parts of the journal still confuse me, but I think it confirms there are many layers to this woman.

Behind her cold exterior Saloni is a caring and tender person. If I had never read the journal, I would never know there was another side to her. She talks about wanting to travel the world to help the less fortunate one day. Sometimes she draws little doodles based on how her day is going. There's mention of wanting to start a family as well. When I read the entry, my chest tightened; I don't know why.

The more I read the stronger the pull towards Saloni gets. I'm getting to know a truly incredible person. I wish I could talk to her but it would be inappropriate, and I could get into a lot of trouble.

There's been no mention of Mr. Fellow, or Mr. Barlowe, in the journal yet. I need to keep reading. There has to be something important in it. I just need to find it.

The reason I'm doing this is to help Mr. Fellow's family put him to rest and to put away the killer. It's my job. Even though my actions are shameful it's for the greater good.

Telling myself this allows me to ignore the elephant in the room. It lets me bury the terrifyingly horrible truth.

I want to see her.

Chapter 8 - Leave Your Shoes at The Door

The pull keeps growing stronger and stronger. So strong even I'm not surprised when my drive leads me to her house.

After we wrapped up the crime scene, the Barlowes were informed they could return home. They didn't go back right away but at the two-week mark they settled back in.

It's been almost 3 weeks since the investigation started. The Barlowes stopped cooperating with us after the press release, hence me testing what little luck I have left in life. I contacted Saloni and she agreed to meet with at her house today on the condition I come alone. Key raised her eyebrow when she heard and told me it wasn't a good idea but otherwise kept her comments to herself.

The drive over is so quiet I can hear my rapid heartbeats and quick breaths. I don't know if Mr. Barlowe will be there or why she agreed to this meeting without her lawyer. What if she knows I took the journal? Will she chew me out? I could get in serious trouble for not logging the journal as evidence.

Most would consider me a calm level-headed guy, but my emotions are running wild right now—hot and cold. I'm afraid but excited. The built-up anticipation in me threatens to burst out. Taking deep breaths I grip the steering wheel. I try to calm my nerves by reminding myself I've spoken to Saloni before. If she does know about the journal, I'll come clean and pray she's merciful.

None of it works. This woman unsettles me.

———

Shortly after I ring the doorbell Saloni greets me. Her hair is pulled back into a ponytail again but this time she doesn't have on makeup. She's in a plain yellow shirt, the kind you could get from Target but

I'm sure it's not, and soft white slacks. The outfit looks casual, but I can tell it's expensive. A bit much for a day at home in my opinion but I guess this is what rich people do.

We lock eyes and I can tell by her raised eyebrows and widening eyes she's feeling what I'm feeling. Because of the circumstances, and environment, of our first interaction there were things I didn't notice about Saloni. This time I noticed more of her features. My initial assumption that Saloni was only Black was wrong. Even without having a closer look at her face this time I should have picked up on it by her name. Saloni is half Indian.

"Come in Detective West. Please leave your shoes at the door." Her voice rings clear and authoritative as if we were in a business meeting.

I pause for a second not expecting the request. My eyes trail down to her fuzzy house slippers. I clear my throat and quickly remove my shoes. Saloni glides across the floor as I follow her into the living room.

"Mrs. Barlowe, thank you for meeting with me today." The house is quiet but still I ask, "Will your husband be joining us?" As I sit in the most comfortable chair, I've ever sat in. It would take me less than 5 seconds to fall asleep—

"No, he's at the office today. Is there something I can help you with Detective?" Saloni's cold demeanor is a stark contrast to the woman on the pages I read.

"Well, we're trying to get more information on the death of Mr. Fellow. If you would prefer to have your husband or lawyer here, we can meet another time… or at the station."

"I can speak for myself. I agreed to this meeting," she snaps.

"Okay. Can you tell me more about your relationship with Mr. Fellow?"

Saloni sighs, "I told you already, we didn't know him."

"Yes, but he worked for you for 5 years. You must have spoken to him at some point during those years."

"Not very much but he and my husband sometimes spoke about sports and other things I'm not interested in." She crosses one leg over the other and checks her phone seeming disinterested.

My spine straightens and I sit up in the chair knowing my next questions could upset her.

"Can you tell me more about your relationship with your husband? Do you have enemies? Is there anyone who would kill Mr. Fellow to hurt you?"

Saloni stares me deep in the eyes and I'm not sure how she'll respond but the gaze slightly unnerves me.

She puts her phone down and responds, "I'm sure you've had a taste of it now, so you know. My husband and I deal with many people in our line of work and honestly, there are probably lots of people out there wanting to hurt us." The ice around Saloni hasn't thawed yet but I suspect it's because of the stress of the last few weeks.

This might be my only chance to speak with her alone. Hesitating won't get me answers, I have to push down any doubts or fear.

"Does anyone come to mind? It could be someone who recently made an uncomfortable comment or sent a threatening letter…?" Saloni shifts in the chair as I list possible scenarios.

"No, I can't think of anyone. I haven't had any disturbances with my patients or staff recently but I'm not sure what goes on in my husband's business. Did you speak with Moriah?"

"Yes, we did, thank you for giving us her contact information. Unfortunately, she didn't mention anything of the sort to us."

"Well, I suppose she wouldn't. I doubt she would ever speak against Yael. No one ever goes against Yael." She uncrosses her legs and wraps a hand around her wrist. With the change in her body language, I sense her walls may be coming down. One more big push is all I need. *Find a way to reach her on a personal level, Izaak.*

"What do you mean?" I ask.

Saloni fiddles with her nails and leans forward in the chair across from me. I lean forward as well. I don't want to miss whatever she's going to say next. She has thick eyebrows and a nose piercing. I hadn't noticed it before because the stud is small. "Can I trust you, Detective West? You seem like an honorable man, but my judgement has been wrong before."

The ice is melting so I forge ahead, "Saloni, sorry if I'm being forward but, please know anything you and I discuss is between us. Okay?"

What am I even saying?

Firstly, she'll probably kick me out for calling her by her first name. And secondly, keeping our conversation between us is not a promise I can keep. I blame my slip of the tongue on shock.

The tension, palpable in the beginning of our conversation, is starting to morph into something raw and uncomfortable like an open wound.

It feels intimate.

A dark storm clouds her eyes. She's not sure what she should say and neither do I. It feels like we're suspended in the moment. This could be it. The moment the façade crumbles and I finally get to meet the real Saloni I've been reading about for weeks.

I hold my breath in anticipation. Saloni opens her mouth to speak but halts as the sound of the front door opening breaks through our bubble. The moment is lost and I feel my chest cave in.

At the same time Saloni's head whips around in the direction of the front door I jump up.

"Sal?" Yael Barlowe's voice booms through the first floor. "Who's here?"

Chapter 9 – No Turning Back

I always knew my luck would run out. There was never much of it to begin with, but this proves to me I should stop trying altogether.

"Yael, I'm in here." Saloni calls out to her husband. She stands up too and we awkwardly wait for Yael to come into the living room.

"What's going on? Why's the detective here?" Yael glances in my direction but the waves of anger flowing out of him are directed at Saloni.

"He had some follow-up questions about Mr. Fellow and I didn't want to disturb you at work." Saloni looks in my direction for support.

"Yes Sir, standard protocol for an ongoing investigation. We haven't been able to get in touch with you guys, but your wife was kind enough to see me on such short notice." This doesn't feel like the best time to extend my hand to Yael.

"You haven't heard from us because you need to go through our lawyers! We're not supposed to talk to you without them. Sal knows better." He heads in her direction, and she takes one small step backward. The change in her persona with me and now her husband makes my jaw drop. This is not the same intimidating woman I know.

The scene plays out in front of me. I watch him stalk towards her with purpose.

Heat swirls in me. The kind which leads to red hot blinding rage. I need to get a handle on this situation. My hands squeeze into fists to regain control and take a deep breath.

"Mr. Barlowe, like I said this was just a standard follow-up. I'm sure Mrs. Barlowe didn't think you or lawyers were needed for something so *rudimentary*." As much as I try to conceal it, my voice is still laced with venom.

"It was not her place." Yael turns to me. "And you need to leave. I will be contacting our lawyers about this."

"I understand Mr. Barlowe. I apologize for the last-minute visit. If there's anything else you think of, please contact us. We will all be happier when this case has been solved." My eyes glaze over at Saloni one last time. Asking her with my eyes if she needs help. As hard as I try, I can't read the expression in her own. It feels wrong to leave her alone with Yael, but I don't have a choice.

"Thank you for your time, Mrs. Barlowe." My eyes pierce her own when I say my final words, "Please contact me at any time."

I mean it.

———

The steam from the hot shower seeps into the bedroom as I throw my clothes into the hamper. I step into the shower, ready to relax after today's events. There's a bit of relief she doesn't know I have the journal, but I left the Barlowes worried about Saloni. I've talked myself out of calling her more times than I care to admit. It even crossed my mind to call from Key's phone but I'm being ridiculous. She has my number.

No call means she doesn't need me.

I was so close! If only he hadn't come home.

Frustration and regret weigh on me as the slam of my wet palm against the shower wall rings in my ear.

Key won't be happy and if Yael follows up with his threat Sergeant Knowles will kick my ass for going to their house. He hasn't said anything yet but there's no telling when he might decide to tell their lawyers. And if the media got a whiff of this I'm screwed.

'Detective visits Mrs. Barlowe in private. Is she having an affair with him too?' I roll my eyes.

But is she okay? I lay in bed replaying our conversation over and over in my mind. There's no way she's involved in Mr. Fellow's death.

After seeing her today, the call is louder than ever tonight. I snag the journal from my nightstand. I'm almost finished. There could still be information relevant to the case in here but either way it doesn't matter.

With the air nipping at me, I paddle the boat
towards the silhouette in the distance.
The choppy sea making the journey difficult
but not impossible.
Her song, using the stars as its source, lights
the path.
There's no turning back.

Propping my pillow up against the headboard I settle in to read. This inexplicable need to know more bewilders me. There's something I'm not ready to confront about what I'm feeling towards her.

———————

My burning eyes focus on the book in my hands. I've been fighting to stay awake for the past hour and a half to read the journal. There was a random entry about a new designer collection recently dropped, more doodles and a short poem about the weather but one entry stood out to me the most. The most recent entry I finished sent a violent chill down my spine. I'm not sure what I just read. It was a poem and in it Saloni mentions an "evil in the house".

Is she talking about a spirit? I don't believe in ghosts, and I don't suspect she does either. Could she mean someone else in the house...like Yael?

When I finally drift off to sleep, I'm still trying to put the pieces together.

Chapter 10 - I'm Not Okay

A week later I finished the journal. Unfortunately, there wasn't any information regarding Mr. Fellow or his mysterious death. I knew this might be a long shot. If she's involved with his murder, I doubt Saloni would put information detailing it in a journal lying around. Not that I suspected Saloni of being the killer anyway.

She might not have known Mr. Fellow well but I believe Saloni is a good person. Some of the journal entries speak about her love for helping people. I assume it's the reason she became a psychiatrist. She never mentioned specific people in the journal but in her line of work I bet it's hard to focus on yourself. With the way it looked the journal could've belonged to a teenager, but I think it was meant to be a place for her to put her inner thoughts and ramblings on paper. There's no way she could hurt Mr. Fellow in a million years.

If only more people could see this side of her – I wish *I* could experience this side of her, not just read about it.

My concern is the evil mentioned in the journal. The only person who comes to mind is Yael Barlowe. He's abusive to Saloni. It's only natural she would think of him as evil.

But does he turn his rage on others?

He seemed nice enough when I first met him, but could he have killed Mr. Fellow?

What would be his motive?

In the past week we got surveillance footage and a log sheet from the community the Barlowes live in. We thoroughly checked the footage and the names on the sign-in sheet. On the night before and during the hours we believe Mr. Fellow was murdered, no one suspicious entered the community. Everyone on the list was either a resident or an employee. Conveniently, the Barlowes' cameras stopped working a few weeks before the murder. They had no footage of their backyard and the neighbors' houses aren't close enough to the Barlowes', so their footage hasn't helped us either.

There was no footage of Mr. Fellow's death or the moments leading up to it.

A deep sigh escapes my lips as I look over all the information we've gathered on this case. There's not a lot. All the leads from Mr. Fellow's family and friends didn't bring any new suspects.

It feels like we're headed to a dead-end, but I can't decide if we should speed towards it or stop and take a break. We could double down on the Barlowes and see what turns up or we could take a step back from the case and let someone with fresh eyes take over.

The clutter on my desk reflects the state of mind I'm in. My shoulders hunch over as I study the examiner's report again. A hand pats my shoulder.

"Come on West, let's go get some lunch," Key pauses and studies my face. "And fresh air."

Looks like the decision's being made for me. Taking a break sounds good. I nod in response and open the drawer to grab my wallet. Before I can grab my keys, my phone screen lights up and starts vibrating. I blink twice, unsure if I'm reading the correct name on my screen.

Key is already heading out the door forcing me to make a split decision. I snatch the phone from the drawer, shout to Key I'll meet her at the car and rush to the bathroom.

The lock on the bathroom door *clicks* as I put the phone up to my ear.

"Hello?" My eyes squeeze shut registering her shaky and uncertain voice. There's a wrench in my chest and I take a deep breath to focus and ease the tension.

"Mrs. Barlow?"

A soft, quiet laugh escapes her lips, "I guess we're back to formalities…"

Is she disappointed?

Ignoring the ache in my chest I ask, "Saloni, what's going on? Are you okay?"

"No. I'm not okay." She pauses and I hold my breath for the longest second. "Yael is out of town for the day, can you stop by?"

The tenderness in her voice is surprising compared to her usual clipped tone.

Is it you, Saloni? I knew you were in there.

Every bone in my body aches to say yes to her but the logical side of me knows this is risky.

"Are you sure this is a good idea?"

"Does it matter?" Her irritation brings back out her façade. This isn't what I wanted. I don't want her walls to go back up. I want to experience the Saloni no one else sees.

What am I even saying? Get a grip, Izaak.

She sighs and the next time she speaks it's in a softer tone. "I just need someone to talk to and you're the only person I can trust right now."

Once again, I'm floored by the pull I feel towards her. Heat rises to my face, and I rub the back of my neck. A nervous tick. *Saloni needs me. She trusts me.* This is not what I expected when I picked up the call, but I know what I need to do.

"Don't move. I'm at the station. I'll be there as soon as I can." We hang up with the promise of seeing each other soon. I splash cold water over my face and hear a bang on the door 'open up'. I mumble an apology to the person waiting to get in and sprint outside to my car.

"Hey West, where are you going?!" Key shouts across the parking lot at me as I unlock my car.

"Sorry! Emergency! I'll text you!" I turn on the car and speed out of the parking lot not sparing Key a second glance.

Chapter 11 - World's Comfiest Chair

Less than an hour later, I'm sitting in the world's comfiest chair across from Saloni. The same spot as last time. The drive felt long, never-ending. I was so focused on getting to Saloni I hadn't noticed when it started raining. There was a drizzle after I left the station, but it turned into a full downpour on my way here—with lightning and thunder setting the ambiance.

When I got to Saloni's I contemplated waiting out the rain because I didn't have an umbrella, but her voice sounded shaky on the phone, and the overcast didn't look like it was going to clear up any time soon, so I ran in the rain from the gate to the front door.

There aren't many lights on but the floor-to-ceiling windows provide natural lighting—except today. The place has a gloomy feel, matching the state outside. We don't get much rain this time of year. The harsh rain beating down on the house doesn't bode well.

Saloni gives me a towel to dry off, but I'm soaked. Goosebumps line my arm and I shiver as my clothes cling to me. This couldn't get any worse. Thinking about my damp clothes wetting this chair makes me shift uncomfortably. The towel is under me, separating me from the chair, but it's no use. It'll soak through.

Please Lord, don't let me mess up this chair. I can't afford to replace it. Maybe I should sit on the floor.

We're in the same position as the last time I was here but something is different. There's a charge in the air but this time it's not us. An even greater storm coming.

Besides a greeting and offering me coffee Saloni hasn't said a word. I'm not sure if I should speak first. We were cut short the last time but Yael's not in town. We won't be interrupted again. *There's no rush* I tell myself as I sip my coffee.

The rain, my soaked clothes, and the AC make this house feel like a freezer. The hot liquid travels down my body, not only warming me up but relaxing my nerves as well. I am highly strung. This conversation will require me to think clearly so I need to calm down.

This goes on for a bit longer but unable to bear the silence any longer I speak.

"Saloni, what's going on? You said you needed to talk."

"I do." She fiddles with her wrist. "It's about Yael. Remember what I said last time? No one ever goes against him."

"Yes, I do." I'm glad we're picking back up where we left off. I leave the floor open for her to explain.

"Well, I meant it. Yael is a dangerous man. He'll do anything to protect his business. I know he's made shady deals with a few of his celebrity clients. I think he helps them bring drugs in and out of the country. He's never explicitly told me but I'm not a dumb woman."

"This is very concerning. We can have another team investigate but this doesn't relate to our current case on Mr. Fellow's." I'm slightly disappointed. A part of me thought I would take home new information to help our case.

"It does," she pauses. "I think Yael killed Cypress."

Lightening cracks the sky and lights up the dark room. The main light source is a dim lamp on the other side of the room. I flinch at the loud boom of thunder a few seconds later.

There's nothing for me to say yet so I keep quiet, waiting for Saloni to finish. I had my suspicions about Yael, but I wasn't expecting this from his wife.

"The evening before we found Cypress, I overheard Yael arguing with him. Apparently, Cypress overheard a business conversation between Yael and Moriah. I didn't think much about it at first because Yael makes a big deal out of things sometimes. When he calmed down, he told Cypress to be here early in the morning to work on the roof. I assumed everything had been settled." Saloni grabs her coffee with unsteady hands. She can barely take a sip because her hands are violently shaking. "I went to bed and when I woke up, I found Cypress downstairs...dead. I think Cypress overheard something he shouldn't have, and Yael killed him for it. When you left the other day, I confronted Yael about my suspicions, and he didn't deny it." Saloni chokes up and tears begin to stream down her face.

Her vulnerability shocks me speechless. Without thinking I lean forward and place my hand on top of hers. She doesn't reject me, so I stroke her hand—silently encouraging her to continue.

"I didn't want to believe it—I couldn't. How could the person I'm married to be a killer? I didn't reach out because it doesn't make sense. Well, I couldn't because he's been watching me like a hawk ever since I told him my suspicions. He told me I was being crazy, and I should stop making up fantasies no one would believe. But with him being out of town for the day, I knew this would be my best chance. He's had this day planned months ago so he couldn't back out of it. Thankfully, it allowed me to reach out to you."

This situation needs to be handled delicately. Saloni's upset and I want to believe her but there are still missing pieces and questions that haven't been answered. She didn't see or hear the murder take place because she was asleep.

"Saloni, are you certain about this? If I take this to my boss, we must be absolutely sure."

"I'm sure, Izaak. Well as sure as I can be. Yael had a motive and no one else was on this property. It had to be him. He wanted to prevent Cypress from going to the police about his shady dealings. Yael is a big man; he could've carried Cypress up to the balcony and pushed him off." She wipes her face with the back of her other hand.

My back hits the chair as I contemplate this information I've been given. Yael had a motive and the means to execute Cypress' murder. It makes sense and it would feel good to close this case.

It took me a while to register she used my first name. If we hadn't been discussing her husband being Cypress' murderer, I would have had a different reaction but right now my focus is Yael.

Besides the sounds of the rain falling it's quiet. Looking at Saloni is impossible. This information is heavy, and I need to figure out our next steps, but there's also a sense of relief. Cypress Fellow would finally get the justice he deserves.

"Izaak…What do I do?" This time Saloni reaches for my hand. I look up and her eyes are still wet with tears. There's no need for me to know what's going on in her head. I know her. She's looking to me for help and even though I don't have all the answers I make a promise to myself to be there for her.

"Okay." I sound more confident than I feel. "Here's what we'll do…"

Part 2

Chapter 12 - A Cheating Jezebel

3 Months Later

After Saloni shared her suspicions regarding Yael's involvement in Mr. Fellow's death, I informed the sergeant and Key. There was no time to second guess. We didn't have any other suspects and the pressure to close the case hastened us. When Yael returned from his trip the next day, we arrested him. I will never forget the crowd of reporters and paparazzi outside of their gated community and at the police station waiting to get a glimpse of the man we believed to be the killer.

The reporters were hungry for the new story. The public assumed Yael killed Cypress because Saloni was having an affair with him. Yael and Saloni didn't make statements during the first week, but the headlines got crazier by the day. They were insatiable.

Social media was even worse. People were making nasty comments about Saloni on the Internet. Even bloggers began sharing their opinions of her. Videos were made involving conspiracy theories about the couple. People began sympathizing with Yael, claiming he was protecting his marriage. They reduced Saloni to a cheating jezebel, instead of seeing her for what she truly was—Yael's second victim.

Saloni chose to lay low with a relative after Yael's arrest but after a week she broke her silence. She returned home and greeted the media with her head held high. She dispelled the rumors she was having an affair with Mr. Fellow, reminded the public not everything you read is fact and gave a brief but encouraging speech to those who could be going through a difficult time as well. Any details surrounding the investigation were not to be shared with the media. She did a good job steering clear of any questions about the murder.

On that day my respect for her increased tenfold.

Sergeant Knowles was ecstatic we were able to close the case. Now we wait for a trial and verdict. Saloni will be our most important witness, but we're sure we can get a guilty verdict regardless. After we received the autopsy report we were able to confirm the cause of death and with Saloni's help piece together what happened. Yael had suffocated Mr. Fellow with a pillow and then thrown his body off the balcony to look like a fall.

Saloni found the pillow in their attic the week after she returned home. She asked me to come over because she was sure it hadn't always been in there. Key grumbled when I asked her to stay behind because Saloni preferred to only speak with me. I took the pillow with me, and forensics were able to match the fibers on the pillow with the fibers found on Mr. Fellow.

All the pieces came together. We have our killer in custody and Mr. Fellow will get the justice he deserves. As a detective this is the most rewarding part of my job. We can't bring back loved ones from the dead, but we can hold those responsible accountable for their actions.

Fortunately, Yael was denied bail so Saloni doesn't have to worry about him having access to her. He's asked to see Saloni many times, but she refuses to visit him. I sleep better at night knowing Yael won't be able to hurt anyone else ever again.

Saloni and I have remained in touch and become close. She's in a fragile place right now and needs a close confidant. She fears one of her friends, or even family members, might leak information about Yael and the case. She even fired their chef and stylist. The paranoia is expected considering what happened in her house and how big the story got.

The past few weeks I've spent one-on-one time with her. These visits had nothing to do with the case. I've even cancelled a few plans with friends when she needed me. At least once a week I stop by her place to check on her, even though it's completely out of the way. After work I stop there before I head home, and Saloni ensures I leave with a plate of food as thanks. There have been a few times I got off early and had dinner there. Regardless of my confusing feelings and the electric charge I know we both feel between us, I have no expectations. I'm here for her as a friend. I'm honored by her confidence and trust in me; I don't want to take advantage of her vulnerability.

Key isn't too happy about this. She thinks I'm crossing a line and doesn't trust Saloni. I agree, I may be crossing a line. The rules surrounding our situation are confusing but I'm sure I'm not winning any gold medals. Regarding Key's distrust…she's never liked Saloni, but I know Saloni better than she does.

When I stop by Saloni it's for her benefit. She's told me multiple times I'm all she has. If I leave her for too long, she won't recover. Considering what she just went through her mental health is very important to me. Right now she needs me, and it feels good to be needed. I can't take away her pain, but I can be there for her.

Getting to know her without all the stress has been a breath of fresh air. I enjoy spending time with her and look forward to our weekly visits or phone calls. She is everything I thought and more. Every word out of her mouth is like music to my soul. She's a complex being. There are many layers to her, and I want to get to know them all.

Am I falling for her?

———————

My phone rings and I smile when I see Saloni's name on the screen. We talk on the phone almost every day. It's not always a long conversation, and sometimes we only say a few words, but it's nice to hear her voice.

"Izaak?" She greets me.

"Hey Saloni, how are you?" I try to mask my excitement but I'm sure she can hear it in my voice.

"I'm okay," she pauses. "I'm thinking about going back to work soon. It's been 3 months; my patients need me."

My mood shifts. "Are you sure it's not too soon?" I ask, voice thick with concern.

"No, it's time. I need to move forward with my life and move on from all this negativity. I'll never be able to if I keep standing still." She sounds resolved.

"Well if you're sure, then I'm here to support you. I think it's a good idea." My concerns don't matter. If this will help her then I'll give my full support.

"Thank you, Izaak, for being here for me these last few months. I couldn't have gotten through it without you. Whenever I need you, you're there. How can I ever repay you?" Her tone lightens. Even though it's been months, I'm still surprised by how genuinely good and nice Saloni is. My first assumption of her was wrong.

"Please Saloni, there's no need to repay me! This is my job, to care about others."

"I think you and I both know you've done more than your job dictates."

I laugh sheepishly on the other end and rub the back of my neck.

"Well, what can I say? You're special." The implication of my words dawns on me. There's no response on the other end and I panic.

Sometimes we sit on the phone in silence, but I worry she's upset. After recently finding out her husband is a killer, I doubt she wants advances from anyone—especially me.

"I'm sorry." I stutter nervously through my words. "I-I just meant—"

"Izaak." Saloni stops me with her commanding voice, and I close my mouth. "It's okay," another pause. "You're special to me too."

The phone nearly slips out of my hand. *What did she just say?*

The feelings I have towards her are wrong. It's unethical and the timing is horrible, but I've never felt this way about someone. I don't know if I ever will again. The circumstances surrounding our situation are reprehensible but she's ready to move on. She just told me herself.

Mustering up my courage, I try my luck one more time. I have no idea what's gotten into me. Izaak is the guy who follows all the rules. A bit naïve but he's an honorable and decent guy you can always rely on. But she makes me not care. Ever since I laid eyes on her I've thrown caution to the wind. I've done so many things I never thought myself capable of. She makes me bold and brave.

After a long pause, I let the next words flow out of my mouth without much thought.

"Saloni, do you have plans this weekend?"

Chapter 13 - Close Family Members and Friends

9 Months Later

It's been about a year since we arrested Yael. My life is so different; I could never have imagined things would change this drastically in a year.

After our first date Saloni and I were inseparable–besides when we were working. We couldn't bear to be apart and when we had to be away from each other we were always on the phone. Saloni would constantly tell me how happy she was to be with someone who understood her and didn't abuse her. The day she said, "I think we're soulmates Izaak. I love you." I knew I would do anything for her. A tear formed in my eye when she bought me a new car for my birthday.

Keeping our relationship under wraps until Yael was found guilty wasn't easy with all the attention on us both but we knew we had to do it. The start of our relationship was unconventional, but it was new. We had to protect it or it would be tainted by others' opinions.

Our relationship hit the news fast but died hard. The public wasn't impressed with me and there was more interesting news than Saloni dating the detective who put her husband behind bars. The comparisons between Yael and me did bruise my ego a bit. Saloni would brush me off and tell me not to give it a second thought.

After the news calmed down, we decided we didn't want to waste another moment being apart. We were spending all of our time together anyway. Saloni paid a lot of money to hire good lawyers to get her divorce expedited. She got the house and most of their assets. Once the divorce was finalized, we got married 5 months later. The ceremony was small, kept to just close friends and family. People thought we were crazy. It didn't matter to us. This is my first marriage and I'm lucky to call Saloni my wife. She's hardworking, independent, strong and a truly caring person underneath it all.

For someone like her to have dealt with so much and still keep living every day to the fullest. Her strength is admirable. Saloni still struggles with what happened to Mr. Fellow. She blames herself for not seeing the evil in Yael because she's a psychiatrist. I remind her it's not her fault and Yael was skilled at hiding his true nature but it's no use.

On these days I try to get her out of the house, take her on dates, get her favorite ice cream, I've even tried taking her down to the shooting range. It's the place I go when I need to reset but no matter the suggestion, she almost always turns me down. During these moods she withdraws emotionally and physically. I feel helpless—unable to say or do what she needs. The journal didn't have enough to help with situations like these and I'm not equipped to deal with emotional trauma of this magnitude. My life is consumed with my job; it's all I know.

When she withdraws, I see glimpses of the stand-offish woman I first met. She can be cold and mean so I give her the space she needs. Within a couple of days she always comes around and then everything is perfect again.

Well, almost everything.

We currently live in her house. The house Mr. Fellow died in. I suggested she move into my place, but she was insistent. Her house is bigger, safer from the public and intruders and she's comfortable there. Eventually, I caved. After everything she went through, I didn't want to cause more stress. When I agreed to live here it came with the condition we would find a new place in the future. Living in the home your wife's ex-husband killed a man in would make anyone uncomfortable.

Then there's the issue of my partner, Key…

"I just don't get it West. One minute you're focused on solving the case and the next you're *married* to the woman!" Key's glaring at me as she raises her voice.

We're in the car on a stakeout for our new case. I'm not the kind of guy who gets loud often but Key has a bit of a temper. I sigh. This isn't the first time we've had this conversation. As a matter of fact, it seems we're always having this conversation. Key doesn't approve of my marriage. I understand it took her by surprise but as my partner, I thought she would at least support me.

"Key, we've been over this. It just happened but Saloni isn't the person you think she is. She's amazing and we're happy. Why can't you be happy for me?" My voice remains calm and level.

"I don't not want to be happy for you but it's just wrong." She turns away from me and faces the steering wheel. "She's not your type. You're into soft, nice girls and Saloni is a cold, frigid b—"

A side eye stops Key in her tracks.

"Sorry, I just don't know her, and you didn't even invite me to your wedding!" She mumbles the last bit and I feel a pang in my chest. The guilt eats at me. Key would have been invited but Saloni wanted to keep the ceremony small to avoid any media involvement. The reasons were sound but regardless, Key's feelings were hurt which is the last thing I wanted to do. She has been my partner and friend for a long time; I know I need to make it up to her.

"I'm sorry, Gray. I told you why we couldn't invite a lot of people," I pause to consider my next

words carefully. "About her not being my type…
there's something I never told you because I wasn't
sure how you would take it." The story of finding the
journal and falling in love with Saloni tumbles out of
me.

Key's mouth hangs open after my confession.
"Wow, Izaak. I didn't know you had it in you," She
says dryly but I know she's joking.

"Oh, shut up," I laugh.

"Does she know you read her journal?" She asks.

"No, I haven't told her yet," I admit. Key gives
me a look of disappointment and I rub my neck. "I
know, I know. I'm starting my marriage with a lie, but
she'll see it as a violation of privacy and will think I
was looking into her as a suspect. Everything's going
well right now, I don't want to mess it up. I put the
journal back after she told me about Yael. She never
noticed it was gone."

"Man, you're playing a dangerous game. What if
someone had found out you took it during the
investigation?" Key shakes her head. "Anyway, I am
happy you're happy, but I wouldn't be a good friend
if I didn't share my doubts."

"I appreciate you looking out for me. I'm sure once you get to know her, you'll like her. How about we plan a dinner soon? And you can bring over whichever lucky lady you're dating now."

Key fiddles with the watch on her wrist, "Speaking of …"

Chapter 14 - You're Not Paying

"Veronica, how are you?" I enthusiastically greet Key's date, Veronica, the Medical Examiner she ghosted. Apparently, after their awkward run-in at the morgue they reconnected. Key hasn't ghosted her yet, so this time seems promising. I'm happy Key is happy and I'm glad she's getting to spend some time with Saloni. Their relationship could use some mending on both sides. Tonight was also a good excuse to come to one of Saloni's favorite restaurants. I enjoy the place myself.

La Ciccia is a small, family-owned Italian restaurant. The couple who owns the place moved to California about 10 years ago. We've been here enough times to have become well acquainted with them. If they're not busy sometimes they will come out from the kitchen and talk with us for a bit. This restaurant is ranked high on my list of places Saloni drags me to. What I love most is the feeling you get when you step inside. The place is homey, and you can hardly find this vibe in other places around here.

"Izaak, it's good to see you!" Veronica gives me a warm squeeze and a light kiss on the cheek.

"Let me introduce you to my wife, Saloni." I turn sideways to give Saloni and Veronica better access to each other. The entryway is not big and today seems a little more crowded than usual. "Saloni, this is Veronica and of course, you already know my partner, Gray Key."

Veronica extends her hands in greeting with a smile and Key waves from behind her. Saloni's reaction is delayed so I steal a glance at her.

My breath catches in my throat. She doesn't meet my gaze and an unsettling feeling washes over me. Saloni hasn't made an attempt to shake the outstretched hand, but her eyes bore holes in Veronica.

The bustling of the restaurant continues as the four of us remain locked in this moment. Saloni's standing as still as a mannequin. I can't tell if she's breathing and there's a dark look on her face. We're all unsure what to do. Saloni wasn't upset on the way here. I don't know what brought this on.

Did Veronica offend her? Did Saloni not want to come to dinner?

It couldn't have lasted more than two seconds, but we all saw it and it plummets the once cheerful mood. Before any of us can react, her lips pull up into a smile and she transforms into her bright and bubbly self. She ignores Veronica's hand and goes in for a hug.

Veronica's apprehensive, but she hugs Saloni back. Key and I make eye contact and exchange a silent conversation while I rub the back of my neck.

Key: What the hell?

Me: I don't know.

"It's nice to meet you," Saloni says sweetly. It's like whiplash.

Worry fills me as I try to process that split second. One of the owners comes out from the kitchen and greets us. I try to brush off the uneasy feeling as we're seated for dinner, but Veronica and Gray are tense. I don't blame them.

"I love this place!" Saloni cheerfully tells the other two. "Izaak and I come here often. It's small and quaint. No one ever finds us here."

Veronica and Key's face morph into various states of confusion.

"She means the media," I clarify, still a little jittery.

"You would think after the case closed they would stop but they still follow us around from time to time. It's annoying." She adds, rolling her eyes.

"That must be tough," Veronica says sympathetically.

"Oh, darling I'm used to it. There has been a lot of press and cameras over the past year I had no choice but to adjust. I work with some big names and have a large following on social media—it comes with the territory. Izaak's had it the hardest, but I've been helping him get through it. I don't know what you would do without me babe." Her fingers search for mine under the table. When our fingers interlock, she squeezes. The small gesture of affection calms my nerves and lifts my mood.

"Yeah, they still come by the station too," Key grumbles. She hates when they show up to hound us with questions about Yael or my relationship with Saloni.

"Veronica, what do you do for work?" Saloni asks taking a sip of water.

"I'm a Medical Examiner. I've worked with your husband and Gray on a few cases. Including Mr. Fellow's." Gray and I exchange glances again.

"Oh, how fascinating." Saloni smiles but the warmth doesn't reach her eyes. The appetizers are placed on the table and the uneasy feeling resurges. It crawls its way to the base of my throat making it hard to swallow. "Excuse me, I'm going to use the bathroom." My wife pushes her chair back and walks away.

When she returns from the bathroom, we order our meals and there's a bit of awkward tension before we're able to settle into a steady flow of conversation.

After a slightly heated debate with Gray on sports, I change topics.

"Want to go to the shooting range next week?" I ask Gray placing my arm around the back of Saloni's chair. We've all had two glasses of wine by now and it's helped to lighten the mood. Saloni's more relaxed and she and Veronica have found common ground in their love for clothes.

"Yup. I love any opportunity to wipe the floor with you." She chuckles and my eyes roll, but I know she's the better shot.

"What?!" Veronica swivels her head to look at us. "Gray, how come you've never taken me to the shooting range?"

Gray's brow furrows. "I didn't know you would be interested V, sorry."

"Well, now you know! You can make it up to me." She winks at Gray and seamlessly continues her conversation with Saloni about designer clothes.

Dinner is delicious and the wine keeps flowing. Later in the evening, both owners come over to our table to say hello and before I know it, we're all laughing— the tension of earlier this evening long forgotten. I lean over and kiss the side of Saloni's head. It would be nice to do this more often because,

91

for the last nine months, when I'm not at work I'm spending all of my time with Saloni.

We're the last to leave the restaurant. Veronica's a little wobbly on her feet as we all hug goodbye and plan our next outing: a hockey game. Even Saloni seemed interested, and she's told me before she's not interested in sports. Throughout the night she was a little withdrawn, but I know she's trying.

———————

The drive home was quiet, but I didn't mind. If Saloni has something on her mind, she'll tell me.

When we get inside, I head straight upstairs to the closet. We're not in the master bedroom. I drew the line at sleeping in the same bed she and Yael slept in. We use one of the other bedrooms because the rooms are so big. Any room could be the master and all the bathrooms upstairs are in-suite. This closet is smaller than the master's but for me it's plenty. Saloni moved most of her clothes over. She had to leave the rest in the other closet because my clothes needed a home too—even though I don't have nearly as much as her.

Saloni follows me in the closet as I begin to undress before taking a shower.

"Are you okay?" I ask gingerly as I unbutton my shirt. It crosses my mind that Veronica brought up Cypress tonight. Saloni could be in one of her moods.

"Yes." Saloni's tone is cold. The moods have been better over the past two months. It was naïve of me to think they were gone. When she's in these moods I stay away. It feels like all her frustration is geared at me. My jaw clenches in irritation. We had a great evening. She didn't make dinner the easiest in the beginning but now she's the one upset. I take a deep breath before responding.

"Babe, what's going on? You acted a little strange tonight and now you seem upset."

"I'm not upset." Saloni unzips her dress and puts it back on the hanger. "Do you think we should have someone re-do this closet? There's not enough space and I want to move the rest of my clothes over. We can knock one of the walls down and take some space from the other room..." She rambles on about the closet.

"Wait Saloni are you sure you're, okay?" I ask. "And isn't renovating a waste of money if we're going to move eventually?"

"I'm fine Izaak!" She snaps. My teeth grind together as we head into the bathroom. "And what does it matter the cost? It's not like you're paying for it."

My feet trip over each other but I manage to stay upright. Yes, it's a fact Saloni earns a lot more money than me because of the social status of her patients. She also got a lot of money in her divorce settlement, including the house, but I didn't expect her to say it so matter-of-factly.

Saloni notices the hurt on my face. She walks over to me and wraps her arms around my neck. "I'm sorry babe. I didn't mean it how you're thinking. I just meant I'll pay for it because I want the remodel. Come on, let's take a shower." She kisses me deeply in apology and gently rubs the tips of her fingers down my neck. "We're so good together aren't we babe?"

My head nods in agreement and I'm lost in her kiss and this moment. And just like that, all is forgiven. My concerns about her behavior tonight vanish. Any concerns I have don't matter. What matters most is the person in front of me. The person who makes my world start and stop with the snap of her fingers.

Saloni.

Reading about her was nothing compared to the real thing. When I'm in her presence the pull is much stronger than when I read the journal.

> *Long forgotten is the fatigue and discomfort from the cold air and water when I lay eyes on her.*
> *The twinkling stars outline her silhouette.*
> *A mystical creature of immeasurable beauty…*
> *waiting for me.*
> *Calling to me from right below the surface.*

Saloni pulls me under the steaming shower head.

Chapter 15 – Safekeeping

"Your grandmother hates me." A groan escapes my lips as we fly down the highway heading home. Saloni laughs at me from the passenger seat.

"Babe, no she doesn't. My grandmother is very old school; she's upset we didn't have a traditional Indian wedding. If it were up to her, we would've had more than 5 wedding ceremonies. Yael and I had 3 to appease her but I'm over it." She swats her hand.

"Is it too late now?" I ask in distress. Saloni laughs again.

"Well, you did want a small ceremony." She says matter-of-factly.

"*Me?*" I turn to her in disbelief. She was the one adamant about a small wedding. A ceremony so small Gray wasn't even invited.

"Even if it isn't, you married me—not my grandmother. We'll attend Diwali with her next year, and all of this will eventually blow over. Don't worry." She interlocks her fingers in mine and kisses my hand. The small gesture releases any tension.

Today was not my first time meeting Saloni's grandmother, but it was the most time I've spent with her. When we arrived at her grandmother's house, she performed the Puja. I have seen Saloni do it before, but watching her grandmother was completely different. I gazed in awe at her devotion and focus. Saloni's grandmother was friendly in the beginning but after we settled in, she was a bit cold and distant.

We ate lunch there. The food was spicier than Saloni's, but it was flavorful. Eating the curried chicken and rice was the only time I relaxed. My muscles were so tense when we left, I felt as stiff as a board. I was afraid I had said or done something wrong.

Saloni looks like a younger version of her grandmother and it's not hard to see where most of Saloni's mannerisms come from either. They're very close which makes her grandmother's approval very meaningful. I hope one day I'll be welcomed with open arms.

———————

Instead of going straight home, we stop by a nearby park. The sound of kids and dogs playing fills the air. There's a small dog park to the left and a jungle gym up ahead on the right as we walk the trail. My reason for wanting to stop was fresh air but I have an ulterior motive. I can barely contain my excitement as we stroll along the park, hand in hand, discussing our future.

"Babe, I think we should move out of California. You hate the media as much as I do. We can find good jobs anywhere. Also, think about our kid's future. I don't want them finding out about Yael and being exposed to everything early on," I admit.

Saloni clears her throat and slows her pace almost coming to a stop.

"Kids? We've never discussed having kids before." We lock eyes and a bit of fear creeps in.

She's right. I rub the back of my neck because the only reason I know she wants kids is the journal. "Uhm, I just assumed we both wanted them?"

"After everything last year with Yael it just hasn't been on my mind." Our eyes stay locked as a flying object, probably a frisbee, zooms by. I don't hide the longing in my eyes. This is what I want– days in the park with our kids. "But I'm not saying no. Just not right now."

I breathe a sigh of relief that kids are not off the table. There's no rush. Saloni is 33 and I'm 30, our window isn't closed yet. "I understand. I'm sorry if I brought up bad memories for you. Did Yael ever want kids?" I ask out of curiosity. Although I hate the guy, I'm not one of those men who get insecure when they talk about their partner's ex. Having her now is all that matters.

Yael being in prison also helps.

"It's okay. He didn't want kids and I'm glad we never did," She replies.

"Me too. I'm not rushing you but it's a conversation I would like to have in the future."

"Okay, babe." She smiles up at me and we resume our pace while I secretly look for the perfect bench. This woman has been through so much, yet she still tries to make me happy. I want to do the same for her, hence the park. There's something I want to give her. She mentioned travelling the world in one of her poems. My gift to her is a bracelet with charms of landmarks around the world such as the Eiffel Tower for Paris, a Pyramid for Egypt, a Sand Dollar for the Caribbean…

When I find the perfect bench, we sit. Following my instructions Saloni squeezes her eyes shut. Her legs bounce up and down in excitement because she knows I bought her a present. My hands shake eagerly as I hold her wrist and slip on the bracelet with a "ta-da!". She's going to love it.

Saloni opens her eyes and looks down at the bracelet. There's no immediate reaction. She studies the bracelet looking at each charm. My enthusiasm begins to dim but then her face lights up and she throws her arms around my neck burying her face there.

"I love it, babe!" She pulls back to give me a quick kiss and thanks me for the gift.

"I want to travel the world with you one day but until then, I hope this will do." I kiss her again and we stroll back to the car.

———————

Saloni takes the bracelet off before stepping into the shower. It sits comfortably in one of her drawers full of jewelry.

She did it to keep it safe, I tell myself. But over the next few weeks it feels like kindling being heated in the pit of my stomach when I notice she doesn't put it on again.

Chapter 16 - Cold and Ungrateful

"Are you serious right now Saloni?" My anger boils over. The kindling is well lit and there's a raging fire in my belly. We're fighting again. It's been like this for weeks. We fight over everything and nothing at all. The arguments start over a small misunderstanding but turn into a vicious back and forth on who is or isn't right.

After I gave Saloni the bracelet things changed. She started withdrawing more often, isolating herself, and I was unable to comfort or talk to her when she got in her moods.

"Izaak," the exasperation in her tone makes me cringe at my name. "You don't listen to me. I tell you what I want but you don't listen!" She shouts.

I pace back and forth in the kitchen while Saloni leans against the counter. "I do listen! I'm always trying to give you what you want. I'm always thinking of new ways to be a better husband to you!"

"Here we go." She throws her hands up in defeat and raises her voice. "Not. Listening. I'm telling you what you're doing is wrong. You don't need to think of new ways to be better because I *tell* you what I want. If you would listen to *me* instead of the voice inside of your head, you would know!"

"You know, Saloni, sometimes you can be cold and ungrateful," I chuckle but nothing is funny. "I gave you the bracelet *weeks* ago and you haven't worn it since. I thought you *loved* it?" My sarcastic tone and out-of-place comment throw Saloni for a loop.

She blinks, "What does the bracelet even have to do with this conversation, Izaak?"

"Because it's what you wanted! I got it because you said you wanted to travel the world!"

"When did I say that?" She asks incredulously.

The words tumble out of my mouth before I can stop myself. "You wrote it! In your journal!" My palm slams on the countertop. Frustration and hurt are getting the better of me but it's too late to stitch my mouth shut. Now my wife is going to hate me for what I've done.

"What journal?" Saloni's nose ring glistens in the light as her nose scrunches up. "The only journal I have is at the office. I keep notes in it for my patients."

"I'm sorry, what? Your journal in the closet." The air is being sucked from the room—or perhaps it's my lungs. Whichever it is, I can't get oxygen fast enough and grip the counter for support.

"What are you talking about Izaak? I haven't had a personal journal since high school! And bringing up the necklace was a low blow. How could you be this selfish after everything I've been through? Just leave me alone." Saloni storms upstairs and a few moments later the door slams.

My grip on the counter tightens as I take deep breaths to stop a rising panic attack. The fire in my belly a short while ago has been stamped out and only its embers remain. The things she said don't make sense. She could've lied because she was embarrassed. The journal did seem a bit childish at times.

There's no way she would've forgotten about it because the last entry was only about a week before Mr. Fellow's murder. But she genuinely looked confused when I mentioned the journal.

What is going on?

Bile climbs up my throat and I run to the garbage bin and dry heave until something comes out.

A thin layer of sweat coats my forehead and I feel nauseous even though I've already vomited. Fear cripples me from moving from my spot. There is no way the journal is not Saloni's. Memories of the last year play in my head—how we met, when we started dating, our wedding night—

Bile rises once more, and I vomit. After my stomach settles, I wash my face at the sink and grab a bottle of water.

My hands shake as I turn the bottle cap. Thoughts race through my mind but the most prevalent repeats itself.

If the journal isn't Saloni's, then who did I marry?

Part 3

Chapter 17 - A Perfectly Reasonable Explanation

The next few days crawl by. Key and I have a new case which means I'm working long hours and coming home late. I step out of the station contemplating what I'll eat for lunch. Fall is here. The temperature has dropped a little but it's not nearly cold enough for a jacket. I take a deep breath and kiss my teeth when I check my phone and there's no text from Saloni.

She's ignoring me. We've hardly spoken to each other since our last argument which has sent me spiraling. In addition to a nagging headache which won't go away because eating three meals a day is no longer a priority, anxiety has sunk its teeth into me and I've been in a sour mood. My only solace is ending every night in the same bed.

Despite this small victory sleep doesn't come easily. Most nights I toss and turn, ruminating on our fight. A constant loop of the events plays in my head and haunts me. It's near impossible to figure out what's going on and I don't have the patience to confront Saloni right now.

If the journal isn't hers—

My brain short circuits whenever I try to process what comes next.

Saloni's the woman of my dreams. The woman in the journal is everything I could want and more. There's no way I could separate the two. Saloni *is* the woman in the journal. She is the love of my life. She is my wife and mother to my future kids. There's no one else for me.

There must be a perfectly reasonable explanation for this. Maybe she forgot about the journal in the haze of anger? Maybe she wanted to upset me so she lied? Maybe these are her notes from work?

Izaak, you're not making sense.

Even in my haze of confusion, I know I can't let this go on any longer. I'm a detective. This is my job. There's no one better equipped to figure this out. A different approach is needed; treat it like a case—gather information, review all the evidence, and draw a conclusion.

I square my shoulders back. The goal is to be calm and patient. I'm ready to tackle this problem head-on and save my marriage.

Everything will be okay. I love Saloni. Saloni loves me. We're amazing together. The journal doesn't matter. We will make it through this.

Thankfully, there are no reporters or media outside today. It's midday, she could be with a patient, but I don't want to waste another moment not speaking. I'm desperate to hear her voice. I need to tell her I'm sorry and I'll do better—be better. I'll forget the journal and promise to listen more. Erasing the image I have in my head of my wife will be hard, but I've always thought there were many layers to her. It's not fair of me to box her into the person I met on paper.

Before I can press the call button, I receive an incoming call from Key. I huff, deflated and annoyed about being interrupted at such an important time but this could be about our current case.

"What?" I greet.

"Uhm. Hello to you too." This is not how I typically answer the phone, so I understand Key's shock.

"Sorry Key, I was just about to call Saloni. Is everything okay? Did you find out something new?" I ask in a hurry.

"It's not about the case but I figured you would want to hear this right away..." Key goes silent.

Why do people pause before saying something important? I hate it.

"Yeah, okay. What is it? Spit it out." I raise my voice.

"So, you know I have a friend at the prison. We went to high school together and we've kept in touch. He was my first boyfriend before I—"

"Gray!" She's testing my last bit of patience.

"Okay, okay! So anyway, this friend works at the prison Yael is at," Key pauses for effect. I hold my breath, not knowing what will come next, "He wants to see you, Izaak."

Even with no expectations I couldn't predict this. My first thought was someone killed him in prison.

Very dark Izaak, but back to the matter at hand.

"He wants to see me?" I ask dumbfounded.

"Yeah, I don't know why but I told my friend I would pass the message along. Yael wants it to be discreet. He doesn't want Saloni to know."

There's a long stretch of silence as I process this news.

What on earth could he want to see me for? We've never had a normal conversation. Why now? He could be upset I married Saloni. Is he going to threaten to kill me too?

A chill runs down my spine and I rub the back of my neck. I'm so caught up in my possible future death by my wife's ex-husband I don't register Key's voice.

"Izaak…? IZAAK!" Her voice silences my inner monologue.

"Sorry. Yes. I'm here."

"What are you going to do?" Key is trying to play it cool but the slight shake in her voice tells me she's concerned. My jaw clenches.

"I don't know. I need to think about it. I'll call you back later." I hang up the phone before Key can respond. I'll apologize later.

Once I'm in my car I punch Saloni's name in my phone. This is not the conversation I planned but I have to tell her so we can figure out what to do together. The call rings once before it's declined. My forehead creases and my lips turn down as I frown at my phone, wanting Saloni to call me back. *She could be with a patient,* I remind myself. Instead of calling back I tuck my phone into my pocket and head over to the sandwich shop nearby.

About 20 minutes after the call my phone buzzes with a text notification.

Saloni: Busy. Talk Later.

Izaak: Okay, call me when you can.

It's important.

I'm disappointed, to say the least. If we could discuss this sooner than later, it would be one less thing on my plate to stress over.

The wrapper of my sandwich crumples loudly in the car as I ball it up. I pick up my phone and scroll in vain, waiting for a phone call I know won't come. It doesn't. After my break I dive into paperwork from our last case to distract myself.

When I finally raise my head above water, I realize it's late evening. My stomach's growling from hunger and my back aches from being in the chair for so long. I snatch my phone out of the drawer but there are no texts from Saloni. Irritation blossoms in me and I make a decision.

Key's phone vibrates and she picks it up to read the text that just came through. Slowly she lifts her head and our eyes meet. We're both wide-eyed. I have no clue what I'm doing but if my wife won't speak to me perhaps, I should talk to someone who knows her.

Izaak: Set it up. I want to meet with
him.

Chapter 18 - From One Puppet to Another

Two days later I'm at the prison for our meeting. Key's friend set up a private room for us. It's cold and suffocating in here. The tension and fear swirling in me has the hairs on my arm and neck standing at attention. My back is rigid against the chair, and my body is stiff. There's a little voice in my head telling me I'm betraying Saloni. I wanted to tell her but I'm still receiving the silent treatment—hence I made a stupid decision.

The man sitting across from me with cuffs on his wrist looks different. The first time I met Yael I was intimidated by his height and size. He struck me as a man who captured the attention of everyone, in any room he walked in. A charismatic and proud person. One you couldn't help but like.

Now, he looks deflated. A shell of his former self. He's still tall and looks like he's bulked up but there's no light in his eyes. The man I met is gone and I'm not sure if anyone's in there. Looking at him for too long makes me uncomfortable and I break contact first.

Key's friend never told her why he wanted to meet, and it's caused me to lose more sleep than I care to admit. I want this to be over as soon as possible but he's not making it easy. Yael and Saloni have perfected the silent treatment. I've never met anyone else who can sit in silence for so long. I clear my throat before speaking, "Yael, you wanted to speak with me?"

Yael stares me down and I see some lights flicker on back there. The look in those dark brown irises shakes me to my core. I've seen it before in my line of work but still each time I involuntarily flinch. The eyes of a killer.

"Yes. Did you tell Sal you were coming?" He asks calmly.

"No." I hate him for calling her by her nickname. He knows we're married, and I bet he's doing it on purpose.

"How is she?" The right side of his lip pulls up in a smirk.

My head sharply twists from left to right and back again. The chair scrapes the floor as I stand up. I will not be discussing my wife with this monster.

"Is this all you wanted to talk about? I'm leaving."

"No, wait." He puts his hands up in surrender. "There's something else… Something important."

"Well spit it out, I don't have all day to waste on you!" I bark out. Sitting back down is not an option, I'm too wound up. *Relax, Izaak.* Losing my last shred of patience and sanity in front of Yael would not be good.

"It was her!" He retorts.

"What are you talking about?" I bang my hand on the table.

There's a knock from outside. Behind me, the guard is looking through the glass window on the door. I take a deep breath and put my hand up to indicate everything is okay, and I don't need backup.

"Speak Yael. What is it?" I brace both hands on the table and lean forward. "Speak now or forever hold your peace because I won't be back."

"You need to be careful, man." Yael lowers his head.

"Be careful of what? Are you threatening me? You must be stupid." The tension and fear I felt earlier has morphed into barely contained rage.

"Would you just listen?!"

"I am listening! You're not talking! You've got 2 minutes and then I'm walking out of here and I'll *never* come back. And I'll make sure you never see Saloni for the rest of your miserable life." I sneer at him.

"Good." He challenges. "I never want to see her again. I hate her. She's an evil—"

"I wouldn't continue that sentence if I were you." I tsk. "I can make your life even worse in here."

Yael sits up straight and I see flashes of life dance in his eyes. "Listen to me, Ivan—"

"Izaak," I correct.

"Izaak… I've known Saloni a lot longer than you. I know her better than anyone. I know her games and

I know when someone's being played. You need to watch out for yourself. I'm trying to help you."

"Help me? Why would you ever help me? Besides don't speak as if you know my wife anymore. You were manipulative and abusive. She's so much better off without you."

He throws his head back and laughs, more like howls. I'm about to punch this freak but if I do the security guard outside will come in and stop our conversation so I bite my tongue as I wait for this show to be over.

After a few seconds of listening to the most nauseating laugh I've ever heard, Yael's eyes pierce my own. My heart beats faster. I can't look away. The room could be on fire right now and I wouldn't know.

He scoffs and his voice lowers, "Now that's funny. Here's some advice, from the ex-husband…"

I sit down, needing something to ground myself to regulate my breathing and heart rate.

"…You are not the first and won't be the last. I loved her like the air I breathe. She gave me life and I would've done anything for her. I *did* do anything for her, but Sal is not the perfect woman you think. She is selfish and cruel. I might be a murderer but the only manipulator and abuser in our relationship was Sal. When she's done with you, she'll move on to the next sucker who falls for her act."

"You're lying. I saw how she reacted to you when you stormed into the house the day I was there."

"Be smart Iva—Izaak. It was all a performance. She handed my ass to me right after you left. It was all her. Sal sold me many dreams to do her bidding then left me in this prison to rot. I bet she told you some sad story about why I killed Cypress." His soft chuckle sends intense pulses of warning through me. Something's coming. I can feel it in my gut. A catastrophe just ahead.

"Stop it. You're the manipulator and now you're trying to turn me against my wife! It won't work!" *You need to leave Izaak.*

Another earth-shattering chuckle. "Deep down, I think you already know. There's something not right with Sal. She's smart and beautiful. She's good at making you feel loved—so loved you think you only need her to survive. She's a psychiatrist for Christ's sake! Don't tell me you're too dumb to realize who was pulling the strings."

Stop it.

"Since I have your attention now, let me tell you the story of how Sal told me to kill Cypress—"

"Enough!" I shout, spit flying from my mouth, as I jump out of my chair. "I've heard enough of your lies. You'll rot in this jail for the rest of your life. Don't ask to see me or my wife again." I turn away and slowly—but with purpose—head towards the door. The last thing I need is for Yael to realize how much this conversation has affected me. *Show him no weakness.*

Yael calls out to me as my hand shakes on the doorknob.

"Here's one clue for you to investigate Mr. Detective. How did Sal know where the pillow was?" He sighs deeply. "Izaak, from one puppet to another, I hope you're smarter than I was."

I yank the door open and quickly exit the room. As the door closes behind me, I hear Yael's laugh. It's like an evil omen.

The slight throbbing in my head indicates the onset of a headache. I'm in deep thought on my way to the car. I would be a fool to trust Yael. He's a murderer who ruined my wife's life. He's the enemy. This was a trick to turn me against Saloni.

I know all of this, yet in the back of my mind I'm chanting:

Saloni didn't do it. Saloni didn't do it. Saloni didn't do it. Saloni didn't...

Chapter 19 – A Detective's Day Off

The day after I saw Yael, Saloni apologized. She put the bracelet I bought her back on and promised we would take a trip when I finished my current case. We 'kissed and made up' but something was off. There was still tension between us. Briefly I thought she knew about my meeting with Yael, but she hasn't brought it up, so I put the thought to bed. I would like to say things went back to normal but that couldn't be farther from the truth.

It's been about a week since I saw him, and I have yet to discuss the details of the conversation with Key. She's curious but she's giving me space and I appreciate it. I've been hesitant to share with her because she and Saloni are in a better place now and I don't want to undo all the progress they've made. Besides we're still working on a case and don't need any distractions. Pushing it off a little longer might be for the best.

If I can even manage a little longer. The sinking feeling in the pit of my stomach grows bigger the longer I suffer in silence. If I don't talk to someone soon, I'll burst. It's hard to concentrate on anything when Yael's words are on a loop in the back of my head:

You are not the first and won't be the last.

When she's done with you, she'll move on to the next sucker who falls for her act.

Don't tell me you're too dumb to realize who's the real puppeteer.

Izaak, from one puppet to another, I hope you're smarter than I was.

Like a hamster on a wheel, there is no end in sight to this hell.

"Izaak?" Saloni calls from the kitchen.

Groggily I get up from the lounge chair I was half reading—half sleeping on, taking my beer with me. Today I'm off and decided to take advantage of the free time with much-needed R&R. Part of the patio is covered and has a cooling unit which makes it ideal to enjoy outside without getting a tan.

The pool area still makes me uncomfortable because it's where Mr. Fellow's body was dropped but it's not the same. Saloni renovated the whole backyard. The floors, furniture, and even the grass was replaced. She said she didn't want any reminders of Mr. Fellow. At the time it made sense, but I wonder...

"Yes?" I slide open the patio door.

"Would you like to go out tonight? I think it'll be nice for us to have some fun." She smiles at me.

"Great idea, babe! Should we invite some friends? I can text Key and see what she's up to tonight."

Her smile falters and she stalks over to me with fire on her trail. "Do you think I want to spend time with your stupid work friends?"

"Uhm—"

"Don't answer. Of course you do. Well, here's the truth Izaak, I don't." She points her finger in my face and pulls her lips in tight to speak. "Don't bring your friends up to me again."

"What is your problem?" My chest starts heaving, building with confusion and irritation.

"All I ever hear about is Key this and Key that, or some other stupid person in your life who I don't care about!" She raises her voice. "I'm sick of it!"

"You've been on my ass for weeks, Saloni." I raise my voice. "Nothing I say is right. I asked a simple question. You could've just said no. There's no reason to be rude and call my friends stupid. Forget it. I don't want to go anywhere with you if you're going to act like this. It's unattractive."

"*I'm unattractive?*" She mocks. "What's unattractive is a man who works day in and day out, barely spends any time with me and when he does, he goes on and on about work and his partner. Which I could care less about because my salary pays most of the bills. And let's not forget you're the kind of man who complains about me not wearing a bracelet I don't like! If I'm unattractive, you're pathetic."

126

I feel like I've been sucker punched—the wind completely knocked out of me. My hand grips so tight around the neck of my beer I might break it.

"My work is important Saloni, you of all people should know! It wasn't very long ago you needed my help for your crazy ex-husband who murdered an innocent man. You seem to have forgotten it was me you came to!" My last sentence booms through the kitchen. We're both silent as I try to regain control and lower my voice. "So, the next time you want to disrespect me, my friends or my job just remember where you would be without me, still married to a murderer or worse – in jail with him." I need to remove myself from this conversation before I say or do something I'll regret.

I march pass her into the kitchen and slam the beer bottle on the island. The empty glass shatters but I don't care. I'm not cleaning it up. Saloni remains quiet as I head upstairs to cool off. Sometimes, I can't believe the things that come out of her mouth.

Pacing the room doesn't suppress the pent-up anger in me that has nowhere to go. I need to get out of the house. First, I'll take a shower and then head to the shooting range. I yank my trunks off and leave them on the bathroom floor, too angry to put them in the basket, and step into the shower. The water is still getting hot as I grab my washcloth and soap. After I wash the suds off my body, I stand under the shower head for a few extra minutes.

My mind replays the past few weeks and I let out a deep sigh. It shouldn't be like this. This isn't the Saloni I know. Yael's words ring in my head: *I know her better than anyone.*

Perhaps he's right and I don't know my wife as well as I think I do because the Saloni I fell in love with wouldn't act like this. The Saloni from the journal—

That's it. The journal. I need to go back to the journal. There's something I'm missing. It must be Saloni's, so I don't know why she'd lie. It was in her closet with her things.

After I dry off, I wrap the towel around my waist. I'll find clothes later. Right now, I need to find the source of it all— what started this journey for Saloni and me. I haven't been in her old closet since I moved in so it might not be in the same place.

128

Saloni hasn't bothered to come upstairs to check on me or apologize. It hurts but it allows me to move through the house with purpose and look for the journal without being disturbed.

The journal is exactly where I left it, untouched. I find it odd, but my mind moves on to other things as I begin flipping through the pages. The pull towards Saloni downstairs is present but it's not as strong.

> *I lean forward, looking down into her black eyes.*
> *She pushes up with reaching arms.*
> *Our greeting a caress.*
> *I seal my fate with a kiss as I let her pull me from the boat.*

Chapter 20 – You're A Good Friend

"*What?*" Key slams on the brakes. Thankfully we're in a parking lot and no one is behind us.

I sigh in exasperation, "He said she told him to kill Mr. Fellow—"

"I understand the words coming out of your mouth but it's not making sense. Why would she do that?" Key's staring me down from the driver's seat. Fully engrossed in our conversation and not paying attention to the car she hasn't put in park.

"Key, either drive the car or park but please, pick your mouth up off the wheel and move the damn car."

"Okay, okay!" She turns the wheel and lets the car glide into a parking spot. I sigh, *we won't get back to the station until late.* "This is serious Izaak." Key rarely calls me by my first name when we're on the job, but I expected this reaction.

"I know. I don't know why he would tell me this. At first, I didn't believe him. He's a murderer. He might be bitter Saloni moved on and is trying to get revenge..."

"And now?" Key whispers.

"I don't know. Things are happening which makes me believe not everything he said was a lie and if he's telling the truth about some of these things, could he be telling the truth about Saloni making him kill—"

"Hold on there, partner. Are you sure you want to continue? If you tell me anymore, I'll have to act. You know that right?"

The bottom of my palms dig into my closed eyes while I contemplate my next move. Key is right, we'll both have to act.

This is my wife we're talking about. The love of my life. The person I planned to spend the rest of my life with, not a murderer. Saloni would never be capable of killing.

How did Sal know where the pillow was?

"My gut is telling me something's wrong. I brought the journal. Here have it." I hand the journal over to Key. "Read it and let me know what you think. I'll tell you the rest after you finish the journal. If you come to the same conclusion after reading it, then we can act. Until then, this stays between us. Sounds good?"

"Yeah Izaak, I got your back. Give me a week—"

"Two days."

"Damn, okay man. I'll try to finish it in two days."

"Thank you, Gray. You're a good friend."

———————

Two days later, we're sitting in the car again. Silence hangs for a moment in the air.

"I don't want to make you feel bad, but how did you not see it?" Key finally asks.

"See what?"

"This isn't Saloni's. Nothing in this journal screams 'Saloni' to me. She would never say this stuff. Did you even bother to compare the handwriting?"

"No, I—" I stutter. "It didn't matter. It was in her room, so I assumed it was her own and Saloni's handwriting does look similar to this, so I never bothered to question it."

"Oh man, Izaak, I'm sorry my friend but you don't know—"

"Don't say it." I stop her. I know what comes next, "you don't know your wife". I don't want to hear it. If I do, I'll vomit again.

"Okay, so what's the other stuff you needed to tell me?"

I relay the rest of my conversation with Yael and my suspicions to her. The biggest red flag was Saloni calling me directly when she found the pillow. If I was working on any other case I would've questioned it, but I was blinded by my feelings for her. When I'm done, I've spared no secret. I offload everything on Key, including the first time I went by the house, intimate details about our arguments and Saloni's strange behaviors since we got married.

"So, what do you think?" I ask.

"I think we need to act. I'm not accusing your wife yet but something's not right. Maybe you should speak to Yael again?"

"No. I'm not speaking to him again."

"He's our best chance of getting more information so we need him, Izaak." She declares.

"You speak to him if you want but I refuse to see the bastard again," I snap.

"Fine. I'll speak to him as soon as I can get a meeting set up. You need to focus on getting evidence. We don't have to take this to the Sergeant yet but if something does come out of it, you'll need concrete evidence."

"What are you saying?" My voice is so low I can barely hear myself.

"Treat her like a suspect. Ask her questions, look for evidence around the house, possibly record her—"

"Record her?!" I ask incredulously.

"Yes, Izaak." Key replies impatiently. "This case isn't officially open. You're her husband. If she sees you putting up cameras inside the house to 'keep you guys safe' she won't question it."

Key has a point and putting up cameras for safety wouldn't be a bad idea regardless.

"Okay. I'll do it." My head hangs low. This is not what I want.

"I know this is going to be tough, but we need to find out what happened and if Saloni was involved in Mr. Fellow's murder. I promise we won't go to the Sergeant unless we have concrete evidence."

"Let's just get this over with," I sigh.

For the next hour we come up with a plan of action for investigating Saloni. This doesn't feel real, and I don't want to believe Saloni is the mastermind of Mr. Fellow's murder but the nagging feeling in my gut won't quit.

Chapter 21 – I Feel Sorry for You

Saloni sighs as she watches me fumble over the buttons on my shirt. I've been struggling with them for the past few minutes and I'm not making any progress. Usually, mundane tasks such as buttoning a shirt are a breeze but with my anxiety being at an all-time high for the past few weeks it's hard to accomplish simple tasks when you suspect your wife was involved in a murder. I groan and curse the shirt. Right now I'm seriously considering throwing it in the garbage and leaving the house with no shirt on because I'm behind schedule. It's 9:30 am. I should've left home over 20 minutes ago but I'm stuck in the closet trying to put on a shirt.

Saloni walks over to me, pushes my hands away and begins putting the first button through the hole. "Izaak, I don't understand why we need cameras inside of the house." She rolls her eyes, securing the last button in place.

"It's to keep you safe. Being exposed to one murder is enough for a lifetime." I kiss the top of her head and rush downstairs to my car.

A few minutes later I park on the side of the road and vomit. The roller coaster of emotions since I shared everything with Key has forced me into a constant state of unease and nausea. The cameras have been set up for 3 days but there isn't anything to report. Saloni hasn't done or said anything suspicious, except when I asked about the pillow…

"Oh babe, quick question. At the station a detective brought something up and I didn't have an answer to give him. They were talking about Mr. Fellow's case and how important your testimony and evidence were to get the conviction. You found the pillow. I remember coming over after you called me to bag the

evidence but how did you know Yael used it to suffocate Mr. Fellow?"

Saloni gave me a strange look before smiling sweetly. "I was just in the attic and saw it. It was strange for the pillow to be there, so I thought it might be tied to the case somehow."

"Hmmm... must have been divine luck because I haven't seen you use the attic since I've moved in."

Her smile dropped. "What's this about Izaak?"

"Nothing. I told you some of my colleagues were speaking about the case and I realized I never asked you about it."

"Well, there's nothing more to tell. Yael used the attic, not me. After he was arrested, I wanted to clear out his things and move some stuff into the attic. I hardly used the attic before, and I use it even less now after a murder weapon was stored in there. Is that all, Detective?" The look on her face told me she was not happy with my line of questioning, so I pivoted.

Changing the topic I take her hand in mine. "Well... if you hate having to look at this place so much, it might be time to start looking for a new home.

We agreed this wasn't going to be forever and honestly, this house kind of creeps me out too."

"Whatever Izaak, do what you want." She yanked her hand out of mine and stormed off.

After she got defensive, I thought it best to avoid mentioning the pillow again. If I push her too much, she could close off from me for good which would hurt our investigation. An investigation I feel physically sick about– hence the vomit.

Key and I are meeting up to discuss her prison visit yesterday with Yael. She hasn't given me any clues on how the conversation went which makes me nervous but there's something else bothering me even more. The number of secrets between my wife and me keeps growing. Not telling her feels wrong. Our marriage won't last if we lie to each other, but I remind myself if she's an accomplice I have no choice. I can't share this with her until I know for sure.

Before my meet-up with Key I have a few stops to make. I'll be speaking with two of Saloni's previous coworkers and a friend from college she's lost touch with. Finding them on Facebook was easy. I introduced myself as Saloni's husband, told them I was planning a surprise for Saloni and I wanted to pick their brains for ideas. They fell for it.

If I was planning a surprise this would've been what I'd have to do because I've only met a couple of Saloni's friends at our wedding. Those friends currently work with her and any time I've asked about them since, she's said she doesn't want to "bring her work home" i.e., hanging out with coworkers outside of work. There's no logical reason for Saloni to keep everyone at such a distance but she barely tolerates Key and wants nothing to do with my other friends either.

"She's good at making you feel loved – so loved you think you only need her to survive."

Yael's voice takes center stage in my brain as I drive to the meet-up with Saloni's old friends. It's hard thinking of her in this way but, I'm starting to question the things Saloni has said or done.

———

The conversations go well with Saloni's ex-coworkers and college friend. In my line of work you learn how to get people to open up, analyze body language and read between the lines. Once they get comfortable it doesn't take long for any of them to open up and tell me what Saloni was like.

Anai, the college friend, said, "I feel sorry for you" and continued to say if Saloni is anything like what she was in college that I married an evil person. At the time the phrase struck a chord with me, but I couldn't remember where I heard it.

The ex-coworkers comments weren't as negative, but they did describe her as cutthroat, ambitious and willing to do anything to keep up appearances.

Saloni having a less-than-pleasant side to her is nothing new, but these comments floored me. Her old friends were so openly negative and I didn't expect it, especially when the prompt for the discussion was planning a surprise for Saloni. They didn't have a lot of good comments regarding Saloni's character.

Deep down a small part of me still hoped the journal was Saloni's. A part of me *needed* it to be her own because facing the truth is hard and I wasn't ready to give up the image of her in my head but after these conversations I knew it wasn't. The woman in the journal wasn't who these people were describing.

The only thought in my mind on my way to Key is:

Whose journal is it?

Key's conversation with Yael lines up with what he told me, but he also gave her more details about Cypress' murder and Saloni's involvement. Cypress overheard a conversation about Yael's business. They got into an argument, but Cypress promised not to tell anyone what he heard. Yael was worried so he told Saloni about the argument, and she said she would take care of it. Saloni asked Cypress to come over a little earlier the next morning to work on the roof. That night before bed she instructed Yael to suffocate Mr. Fellow and throw him from the balcony to make it look like a fall. They prepped throughout the night and by morning Yael was ready and waiting for Cypress.

When they realized they wouldn't get away with Cypress' murder Saloni convinced Yael she would pull strings to get him out of jail early. She promised to stay by his side while he was in jail and would wait for him to get out. Once Yael realized she went back on her promise he found a way to get in contact with me. According to what he told Key, he went along with Saloni's plan because he was afraid Cypress might go to the police about his shady business dealings.

I'm sure he regrets the decision now.

Yael also opened up a bit to Key about his relationship with Saloni. He said when he met Saloni, he never would've predicted this is how their relationship would turn out. The verbal abuse from Saloni had been going on for a while but Yael put up with it. Based on what Key shared Yael put up with a lot, including sacrificing having kids because Saloni didn't want them. This confession threw me off because Saloni told me Yael didn't want kids. I don't know what to believe. Yael's a murderer but Saloni has been keeping things from me. I can't trust her and there's only one way to clear all of this up for good. Confront her.

Chapter 22 – Men Can't Do as They're Told

"Are you sure about this Izaak?" Key asks as I park in the garage.

"I'm sure. We're doing this tonight." I say with finality. No time to second guess, I hang up my phone and step out of the car. The sound of my powerful strides towards the house steadies my racing pulse. Key's car is parked close to my house. The wire on me will let her hear everything said between Saloni and me.

We came up with a plan a few days after Key spoke with Yael. Key and I both paled when she told me about her conversation with Yael. She thought he was telling the truth, but we still had no proof. We won't be able to use the wire recording, but I need to know. If I wait any longer, I'll go crazy.

When I enter the house the scent of food permeates the air. *Saloni's cooking?* Since we've been arguing she hasn't cooked as often, and something about this small act causes me to hesitate. My steps become less confident as I walk towards the kitchen.

There's a war going on in my head. This woman could be a cold-blooded killer, but I love her. I walk up behind her, wrap my arms around her waist and kiss the top of her head. This might be the last time I get to be with her in this way. The last time I'll be able to truly love her before everything changes.

"Hi babe, I'm almost done cooking, hope you're hungry for butter chicken." She smiles as she stirs the rice. I wish I could freeze this moment.

"I'm starving," my belly growls as the scent of spices fills my nose. "But we need to talk."

Saloni sighs, "Okay I'll turn the chicken down low, what's going on?" I step back as she turns around after adjusting the temperature on the stove.

"It's about Yael. He asked to see me a couple of weeks back," I confess.

She freezes. Her mouth slightly drops open and her eyes bulge. She didn't expect this to be the topic of discussion before dinner tonight.

"What?" She snaps. "Did you go to see him? And why are you just now telling me?"

Shame washes over me and I rub the back of my neck, unable to look her in the eyes. "Because you were still giving me the silent treatment and I needed to look into some of the things he told me."

"Izaak, this doesn't make any sense. What could Yael possibly have to tell you that you needed to 'look into'? Is this why you've been acting so weird lately?" There's a small line of sweat forming on Saloni's forehead but in her defense the room does seem to be getting hotter. My palms feel clammy.

"Saloni, is there anything you need to tell me? Tell me now and we can fix it. We can make it work, whatever it is." In a last-ditch attempt to save my marriage, I ignore her questions and appeal to Saloni's love for me and give her an out— forgetting Key can hear everything. "Whatever it is, I'll forgive you. Always. Just trust me."

147

"Izaak, I'm losing my patience. I don't know what you're talking about, and I'm very upset with you for seeing Yael without discussing it with me first." She crosses her arms over her chest.

"Did you tell Yael to kill Mr. Fellow? Were you—" I pause, trying to force the words to come out, "—his accomplice?"

Saloni turns around and turns the stove off. With her back to me she whispers, "Why would you ask me that?"

"Yael told me you orchestrated the murder and convinced him to take the fall for it."

"You would believe a murderer over your wife?" Her voice is so low I can barely hear her.

"I'm asking you a question. I haven't made any accusations, yet." My tone comes out clipped.

To her it might seem like I'm calm and have it together but on the inside there's a storm raging, and something inside of me is shattering. My sanity is holding on by a thin thread. Naively, I thought she would take the out and come clean. If she did, she would go to jail but I would still love her. I'm not sure what would happen to our relationship, but I would be willing to try. Sadly she didn't and now, it's too late. She's not who I thought she was, and I need to accept it.

Yael's laugh echoes in my head. *When she's done with you, she'll move on to the next sucker who falls for her act.*

This is not the time to be hearing Yael's voice in my head. I take a deep breath and harden my emotions so I can get through what's about to happen next.

She whips around with tears in her eyes, "You're the detective, right? You tell me!"

"Saloni—" My nerves of steel crack when I see my wife in tears.

"Don't." She puts up her hands up to stop me from coming closer and laughs. "I can't believe that idiot. After all I've done for him… Oh well, I can see in your eyes you don't believe me."

"Saloni, please, tell me it's not true. Tell me you didn't have anything to do with Mr. Fellow's murder." I beg.

"Will it make you feel better?" She wipes the tears from her eyes. They're completely dry now. I cringe at the shift as her lips straighten and face relaxes. The sad woman act is over and the best way to describe Saloni right now is indifferent. To be on the receiving end is a dagger to the heart.

"No, I just want the truth." My hands shake and sweat drips down my body.

Deep breaths Izaak, deep breaths.

"The truth, my dear Izaak, is men can't do as they're told. Absolutely useless. Yael wants to hurt me, so he shared my dirty little secret with you."

"B-But, why Saloni?" I stutter. "And why me?" My body shudders in horror.

"Because Cypress Fellow heard something he shouldn't have. And as for you, my sweet Izaak..." She steps towards me and rests her hand on my cheek, I lean into it and relax without thinking. "I knew you would either be my saving grace or my downfall. Either way, I liked the uncertainty of not knowing. I love challenges."

My body goes rigid in her hands. Fists ball together as I try to control the wave of emotions threatening to crash into me. I lift my head back up and step out of her reach.

"Did you ever love me or was I just a good cover for your murder?" I want to hear it from her mouth. I want her to look me in the eyes and tell me.

"Honey let's not go down that road. I don't think you'll like the answer." *Who is this person?* There is no love or affection in her eyes. She means everything she's saying. I expected this but still, it hurts.

"You know I'll have to take you down to the station, right? You need to answer for your crimes." I try to make my voice as calm and indifferent as her own, but I fall short.

"Crimes?" She laughs. It's a cold and sinister laugh which makes me flinch. While I listen a revelation hits me. After speaking to Saloni's college friend, something stuck with me, she called Saloni evil and now I realize why the phrase stayed with me. In the journal, the person mentioned an evil in the house.

It wasn't Yael—it was Saloni.

Chapter 23 – It's Too Late

"Yes, your crimes."

How did I not see it before? I shake my head in disgust.

"Where's the evidence? I haven't admitted to anything, and you won't get me to write a confession for you." Saloni challenges.

"That's okay. Yael's testimony, character witnesses, including me, an officer of the law, and the tapes from the videos I have set up inside this house should be enough to at least get us in front of a judge and then the jury can decide what to do with you. It's over Saloni."

Desperation flashes across her face, "Wait a minute, Izaak. You can't be serious." Her eyes water as she turns her sad act back on, "How could you do this to me?"

"Stop. You're not fooling me. I really do love you. I even tried to give you an out! We could've figured something out, got you a good deal—"

"A deal?! Come on baby, why not? You know I'm a good person." She carefully walks over to me with a look I know all too well. My siren's trying to seduce me.

> *Our kiss deepens as we plunge downward.*
> *Here is where I want to be– trading the night sky for the dark blue sea.*
> *Until she pulls away from our kiss and unease grows.*
> *The song ended and so will my life if I don't fight.*
> *With an aching heart, I claw back to the surface.*
> *Never to return to her tender arms.*

She halts when I put my hand up to stop her approach, it won't work. "It's too late Saloni. You need to come with me to the station. If you don't, I'll get the police to pick you up which will make a scene. I doubt you want the media seeing you come to the station in handcuffs." I feel a small surge of pleasure at the idea of her being exposed for who she truly is.

"Okay," she sighs in defeat. "Give me a minute. Let me grab my bag and then I'll go with you."

"I'll wait for you by the door." The least I can do is give her a minute to collect herself. Turning around, I exit the kitchen and head to the front door. I'm doing the right thing, but I still feel sick about taking my wife to the station.

Before I reach the door, I feel a sharp pain in my mid-back. A second later, a release and then a *whoosh* of hands and there's another, what I can only describe as, a jab. My knees hit the floor.

Saloni stabbed me, twice.

Her scream pierces my ears as she lifts her hands again to swing the knife down on me. *Stab.* "THIS IS NOT THE END."

I struggle to whisper Key's name before I fall flat on the ground.

"…NOT GOING TO JAIL, IZAAK!" *Stab.*

The wounds aren't deep. It feels like a small knife, but she's stabbed me four times. Hopefully, Key hears what's going on and is already on the way; I don't know if Saloni will stop before she kills me.

She straddles my back, and I focus on her sobs and shouting. There's a shift above me and I know she's bringing her hands back above her head to swing down again. My energy is draining quickly, and I mumble the only thing I can right now.

"Saloni, please," *stab*. "…I love you".

"I'm sorry, I'm sorry, I'm sorry…" She chants monotonously. She sounds detached—far away. As if what's happening isn't real.

My vision blurs. She doesn't take the knife out this time. There's a *boom* close by and the door swings open.

"GET OFF OF HIM AND PUT YOUR HANDS UP…"

Thank God, Key came I think to myself as I pass out…

Part 4

Chapter 24 – I Called Your Parents

The beeping of a monitor wakes me as a stinging pain radiates down my back. Key sits in a chair to my right, and I expect to see Saloni on my left, but the brief confusion passes when I remember she's the reason I'm in the hospital. My wife stabbed me in the back 5 times.

"Glad you're awake." Key leans over and smiles at me. "I called your parents—"

I groan.

"I know, but they had a right to know. They're on their way and should be here tomorrow. It was the first flight they could get out on short notice." I nod my head because I'm not ready to speak yet. I haven't seen my parents much since my wedding. We aren't very close. They don't agree with my choice of career, but I guess when your son gets stabbed by his famous wife, you rush to his side to make sure he's okay.

"The doctor said you should be out of here in a few days. Your stab wounds weren't too deep and didn't hit any major organs or arteries, so they didn't do surgery but want to keep an eye on you just in case."

Using my hand I attempt to adjust myself to a seating position and fail at suppressing a howl.

"Izaak, do you need the nurse?" Key panics.

My head shakes, but Key ignores me and calls for the nurse. The nurse rushes in and helps me sit up then gives me a cup of water. When she leaves the room my eyes turn to Key, ready to get some answers.

"Saloni?"

Key sighs, seeing the resolve on my face. I won't stop until I get an answer.

"She's at the station right now. When I realized she was stabbing you, I called for backup and an ambulance and then I busted in. When I saw you on the ground, I lost it...I almost shot her. I'm sorry I

156

didn't come sooner." Key's voice is thick with unshed tears.

"Gray, you did the right thing. Thank you. I'm alive and I'm glad you didn't shoot her." I reach for her hand and give it a reassuring squeeze.

She smiles at me before her face turns serious again.

"Your bride isn't having a good day. The press is tearing into her, and the public is loving the scandal. It's on every news station if you want to see it."

"Not right now. How is she?"

"Izaak, listen, I heard everything you said to her in the house. I know you love her, but she tried to kill you. You need to let it go man."

"I will, in time, but until then how is she?"

"She's in shock. I still can't believe she stabbed you," Key shakes her head as if she can erase the memory, "but she confessed to everything, including being Yael's accomplice in Mr. Fellow's murder. She's got a good lawyer, so she'll probably get a deal, but she'll be in jail for a long time."

I lean my head back, wincing at the pain as my eyes find the ceiling. "I thought I would be happier about getting justice for Mr. Fellow, but I feel hollow." The confession slips out. My eyes mist over as I try to fight back the tears but it's no use. They're going to spill over.

Key squeezes my hand, "I'll give you some space. I'll be back later."

"Wait." I collect myself for one last important question before I let myself break. "Who do you think the journal belongs to?"

Dark brown eyes open wide. "I forgot about the journal! Wow, um…if it's not Saloni's it has to be someone else who had access to the house. We can ask one of the people we first interviewed who worked for Saloni and Yael?"

"Okay, thanks again, Gray. See you later and give me a heads up before my parents get here." She chuckles and waves while leaving the room.

The door closes and there's a few seconds of complete silence before the tears resurface.

Not only did I marry someone I didn't know, but she turned out to be a murderer and tried to kill me.

This is great. Your luck has finally run out, Izaak.

A humorless laugh is the only sound in the room as I grieve the love of my life.

My marriage isn't my only concern. I may not have a job to go back to. Being married to a killer will not go over well with the Sergeant. I'll be a laughingstock in the department...Maybe I'll move and hope no one will recognize me in a small town. It sounds great but running's not my style. They'll have to kick me out if they want me gone.

After cleaning up my face I turn on the TV. Key wasn't lying, every news station is talking about Saloni.

"We have confirmed she stabbed her husband multiple times..."

"Saloni has ruined the lives of both her husbands..."

"...Ex-husband to give testimony in trial..."

"Detective's wife stabs him..."

After clicking through a couple more stations I turn off the TV. I expected to feel relieved seeing Saloni exposed but there's no satisfaction, only sadness. Too much for me to bear right now so I lay back down to sleep. The nurse adjusted the morphine earlier to make me comfortable. It must finally be kicking in because moving didn't hurt as much the second time.

Saloni is still on my mind as I drift off to sleep.

Chapter 25 – Before I Leave It All Behind

A week later I was released from the hospital. Key visited often while I was in recovery. She gave me updates on what was happening with Saloni. Hearing her name still leaves an ache in my chest. My parents flew in and stayed for 2 days. Once they saw I was alive and well, they headed back home. It was best for everyone.

The doctor told me to take it slow and get rest but I'm itching to get back to work. Sitting around in the hospital for a week left me with too much time to think about everything. My mind kept replaying moments with Saloni over the last year. I spent most of my time alone, thinking about her but there was one other thought gnawing at me; finding out who the journal belongs to. After a week of thinking about it I have nothing.

Instead of resting I would rather be focusing on a case, but the Sergeant ordered me to take another two weeks off. So here I am, at the house, packing up my things. This doesn't count as resting but I need to keep my hands busy. I'm not lifting anything heavy, just packing away some clothes. I've already hired a moving company for next week when I move into my new apartment. Key offered to let me crash at her place in the meantime, but I didn't want to be a bother. Horrible things happened in this house but there were good memories too. Even though it wasn't real, I wanted to indulge in those good memories and wrap them around me like a blanket one last time before I leave it all behind.

The blood—my blood, had already been cleaned up when I got back home. I assume it was Key's doing. I'll have to do something nice for her soon. She has been a solid friend throughout all of this.

She helped me find a divorce lawyer and contacted the chef who used to work for Yael and Saloni while I was in the hospital. He's stopping by the house today. I hope he can help me figure out who the journal belongs to.

I make myself busy with packing and light cleaning for the next two hours while I wait for him to show up.

———————

Two hours later, I'm sitting in the living room having a deep conversation with Lazer Jing, the chef, about food and how he got into the culinary arts. He tells me of the places around the world he's traveled to cook and the celebrity couples he's cooked for. He's currently working for another rich couple in California but plans to open a restaurant one day. It's inspiring to hear him talk about his passion and he strikes me as a humble man.

"So, my friend, enough about me. Was there something you wanted to discuss?" He asks.

"Yes, one second." I grab the journal from the study and bring it back into the living room. "Do you know whose journal this is? I found it in the house a while back."

"It's not Mrs. Bar—sorry your wife's?"

"No, it's not her own. I was hoping you could help me figure out whose journal it is so I can return it to them."

"Let me see it?" He stretches out his hand and I place the journal in it. He flips through the pages looking thoughtfully at the writing.

"I could be wrong but this might be Dixon's. She was Saloni's stylist and one of the few to have a key to this place. I haven't seen her since working here but I think her handwriting is similar. We would pass each other often while working for Saloni and Yael. I always liked her. She had such a nice spirit, very friendly."

"Do you have her contact?"

"I have her on Facebook and a phone number."

"I'll take both, thank you so much, Lazer." Placing the information in my phone I try to stay calm. Lazer and I speak for a little while longer, but he eventually leaves to get back to work. I can only hope my conversation with Ms. Dixon is as fruitful.

Chapter 26 – My Lucky Day

The past two weeks have been hard. I've been debating whether I should see Saloni or not, but I don't think I can face her. My pain is still too raw and intense. I'm scared. Scared I'll fall for her act, again. Scared she'd work her magic and put me under an even deeper spell this time. The thought of it makes me ill. It's for the best I stay away.

As the movers are unloading boxes of my life into my new apartment my phone pings. I see Ms. Dixon's name on my screen and quickly swipe my finger across the screen.

WD: Hi, Izaak. Yes, I remember you from the investigation. Sure, we can meet. Is this about the investigation? I thought the investigation was over.

IW: Yes, it is. This is regarding something else. Let me know what date and time works best for you.

WD: I can meet tomorrow at 3 pm. I'll send you the address of a Starbucks nearby, we can meet there.

IW: Sounds good, see you then.

There's one more ping from Ms. Dixon reacting to my message with a thumbs up. I'm in a good mood. Even if she isn't the owner of the journal, she might be able to help me find the right person. I'm headed in the right direction, and I always get excited when chasing a good lead. Tomorrow, I'll have answers. I'll be steps closer to getting the closure I need.

I rub the back of my neck thinking about how foolish I've been. Saloni manipulated me. I was blinded by her love bombing and thought I knew her because I found the journal. If I wasn't so naïve and thinking clearly, I would've seen Saloni and the woman in the journal could never have been the same person.

———————

The next day I head over to the Starbucks location Ms. Dixon sent me. The journal is in the passenger seat next to me and I swear it's pulsing like a beating heart. Like the heart in my chest beating so fast I can hear it in my eardrums. I turn the AC temperature lower to stop myself from sweating on the torturous drive over. My hands are slightly shaking as I drum them on the steering wheel.

The worst part is I don't know what to say to her. How do you tell someone you read their journal and projected them onto another person who you fell in love with?

It sounds insane. Perhaps I should be checking myself into a facility.

Briefly, I think about turning the car around instead of parking but I don't want to stand her up, so

I muster the last bit of courage I have and head into Starbucks.

I haven't had any lucky days lately, but I desperately need one.

When I step into the building, I spot her in the far-right corner sipping on a drink. She stands up to shake my hand when I approach the table.

"Nice to see you again, Izaak."

"It's nice to see you too, Ms. Dixon." I plant myself in the seat and the chair scrapes the floor as I scoot forward.

"Please, no need to be formal. Call me Wynter. What can I do for you?"

"Actually, I think I have something for you. Is this your journal?" I place the journal on the table between us.

"Oh, my goodness! Where did you find this? I've been looking all over for it!" She grabs the book like it's her long-lost friend. There's a heavy feeling in my chest.

It's not Saloni's.

This is it. The moment I've been waiting for but it's bittersweet. There's a little relief now since I've found the owner but a lot of pain. Wynter is a nice person, but I've been stuck in denial for too long to feel happy about this. I'm a naïve coward who can't handle the complex emotions swirling in me or take responsibility for my part in all of this. Over the past few weeks self-loathing has come in waves and right now I feel a big one forming.

Not here. Not now, Izaak.

Wynter doesn't deserve this. She did nothing wrong and I should attempt to make this meeting pleasant for her sake. My eyes meet Wynter's, and I look at her as if for the first time. Her dark brown skin compliments her light brown curls with blonde highlights. I remember this from the first time meeting her. The curls hang loose around her face today. She has thick dark eyebrows and perfectly, straight white teeth. Her style is a bit edgy, but she pulls it off in the best way possible.

"It was at my—Saloni's house and I wanted to return it."

"Wow, I never thought I'd leave it there! Thank you so much for returning it! I started a new one but—Wait. Did you read it?"

Rubbing the back of my neck I shake my head yes. She covers her face with the book.

"I'm mortified. The whole thing?" She squeaks.

"Yes, I'm sorry. I read it thinking it was someone else's. I wanted to get to know them better…" The lump in my throat forces me to stop.

Wynter moves the book from her face and studies me carefully. "You thought it was Sal's, huh?"

I look down at my hands in shame.

"I'm sorry if that was rude of me to ask. Forget it. I'm just glad I have this baby back. MWAHH!" She kisses the book and beams at me.

For the first time in two weeks the pain dulls a little. Her aura is so bright, it's blinding, but I could use a bit of sunshine right now. There is something special about this woman. She's charming and I can tell she has a magnetic effect on others. Not in the same way Saloni affected me. This pull feels safe, not dangerous.

"How can I repay you?" She asks.

"Please there's no need," I shake my head, "I just wanted to give this back to its rightful owner."

"Come on, at least let me buy you a coffee. I don't have any other plans today. It'll be my treat and then you can tell me all about why it took you a year to return this." She winks at me and heads over to the counter to order a drink. She didn't even ask for my drink order but I'm too tired of everything to be upset. It takes a lot of energy to hate yourself but being around her distracts me and I'm not ready to go home yet.

Wynter saunters back over, a cold, foamy drink in hand with lots of whipped cream. She places the drink in front of me and I can't control the bellyaching laugh spilling out. It's the first time I've laughed this freely in months. There's been so much stress, anxiety and pain—no room for joy. I would never order this drink, and I hate whipped cream but none of it matters when I take a sip of the sugary goodness in my cup.

White teeth flash against dark brown skin and she says, "Now, I've got you where I want you, spill it!"

Today is my lucky day.

The End

The Siren's Song

Her song travels far across the sea to where I stay, safe in the sand.
I know what sirens do; I should be afraid.
But as her song surrounds me, my feet slowly make their way towards the shore.

A dark night blankets the sky as cold sand tickles my toes.
It's impossible to see her in the distance, but her sweet melody propels me forward.
When my feet meet the shore, I barely feel the bite of the freezing water.
The bobbing boat in the shallow is my ticket to her.

With the air nipping at me, I paddle the boat towards the silhouette in the distance.
The choppy sea making the journey difficult but not impossible.
Her song, using the stars as its source, lights the path.
There's no turning back.

Long forgotten is the fatigue and discomfort from the cold air and water when I lay eyes on her.
The twinkling stars outline her silhouette.
A mystical creature of immeasurable beauty…
waiting for me.
Calling to me from right below the surface.

I lean forward, looking down into her black eyes.
She pushes up with reaching arms.
Our greeting a caress.
I seal my fate with a kiss as I let her pull me from the boat.

Our kiss deepens as we plunge downward.
Here is where I want to be— trading the night sky for the dark blue sea.
Until she pulls away from our kiss and unease grows.
The song ended and so will my life if I don't fight.
With an aching heart, I claw back to the surface.
Never to return to her tender arms.

Notes:

The Siren's Song is a poem/ short story within *The House Behind the Walls* depicting Izaak's relationship with Saloni. Throughout the book, Saloni is compared to a siren and we see she has a strong hold on Izaak. He feels this way towards her because she manipulated and tricked him into falling for her. Although he saw red flags in the beginning, he couldn't help falling for her because she was good at showing him another side of herself. When Izaak finally sees her true nature, the spell wears off and he has the courage to leave and never look back.

Acknowledgements

First and foremost, a special thank you to my parents for allowing me to dream and pushing me to achieve my goals. I absolutely wouldn't be able to do this without your love and support.

This book is dedicated to my nephew, Isaac. Thank you to one of the strongest women I know, his mom, for allowing me to create this character. Isaac will live on in our hearts forever.

Thank you to my friends for allowing me to rant about my books and use them as a sounding board. I'm grateful to have a community that supports me.

It takes a team to write a book. I may put the words on paper but without the help of others my books would never be published.

Thank you to Tylen Perpall for bringing my idea to life, not once but twice. I'm sure there are times you hate my nitpicking, but you always come through and create such beautiful covers for my books.

To my editor and beta readers, your contribution to this book doesn't go unnoticed. This book would not be what it is without you. Your honest reviews, constructive criticism and suggestions take my book to the next level.

Thank you to everyone who supports The House Behind the Walls and me as an author. We are just getting started.

About The Author

Native to The Bahamas, Aliyah A. Symonette was born in 1996. In 2014, she moved to the United States to pursue a bachelor's degree in economics and a minor in public health at the University of South Florida. Her love for reading and writing would lead her to publish her debut novel *Norfolk Street* in October 2021. Currently, Aliyah resides in Tampa, FL, where she spends most of her time reading, writing and watching anime and true crime shows.

For more on the author, visit www.pinkletters.net.

Made in United States
Orlando, FL
28 April 2025

60840167R00111